GIRLS
TO THE
RESCUE
BOOK #3

*Tales of clever, courageous girls
from around the world*

EDITED BY BRUCE LANSKY

Meadowbrook

Distributed by Si
New Y

D1041685

Library of Congress Catalog Card Number: 95-17733

ISBN # 0-88166-275-5
Simon & Schuster Ordering # 0-671-57439-6

pp. 1 and 75 "Hidden Courage" and "Cloudberry Trifle" © 1996 by Martha Johnson; p. 13 "Emily and the Underground Railroad" © 1996 by Joanne Mitchell; pp. 27, 53, and 85 "Sarah's Pickle Jar," "Kamala and the Thieves," and "Maya's Stone Soup" © 1996 by Bruce Lansky; p. 33 "Bai and the Tree of Life" © 1996 by Anne Schraff; p. 39 "Young Maid Marian and Her Amazing, Astounding Pig" © 1996 by Stephen Mooser; p. 63 "The Pooka" © 1996 by Jack Kelly; p. 95 "Annie and the Black Cat" © 1996 by Helen Rames Briggs.

Published by Meadowbrook Press, 5451 Smetana Drive, Minnetonka, MN 55343.

BOOK TRADE DISTRIBUTION by Simon & Schuster, a division of Simon and Schuster, Inc., 1230 Avenue of the Americas, New York, NY 10020.

Editor: Bruce Lansky
Coordinating Editor, Copyeditor: Liya Lev Oertel
Production Manager: Amy Unger
Production Assistant: Danielle White
Cover Designer: Nancy Tuminelly
Cover Illustration: Gay Holland

99 98   10 9 8 7 6

Printed in the United States of America.

Dedication

This book is dedicated to my daughter, Dana. I used to make up stories for her when she was young, hoping to inspire her to believe in herself and to pursue her dreams. It is in that spirit that I have written and collected the stories in this series.

Acknowledgments

Thank you to all the young women who served
on a reading panel for this project:

Stephanie Adams, Ana Bascuñan, Valerie Breault, Bailey
Campbell, Ashley Collier, Ashlie Dufour, Emily Ederer, Janeese
Ellis, Amy Finnerty, Allison Garnett, Roberta Georgerian,
Amanda Griffin, Jennifer Guptill, Jenifer Hamilton, Haley
Hastings, Elizabeth Holmes, Vanessa Hoza, Amanda Johnson,
Jamie Judson, Jenney Kirby, Monica Lee, Lauren Lieppman,
Brittany Martinez, Ashley Nobles, Amy Norris, Jennifer
Owsiany, Michelle Renee Panethiere, Amber Nicole Penrose,
Stephanie Phillips, Cassie Powers, Jamie Radford, Kiera
Reinsch, Melissa Roberts, Amy Seubert, Bailey Summers,
Kristin Webb, Emily Winters

Contents

Introduction

The response to the first two books in the *Girls to the Rescue* series has been overwhelmingly positive, from girls, parents, teachers, booksellers, and reviewers. I have continued to write and search for new stories and we are trying to expand the series as fast as we can.

While traveling around the country to bookstores, schools, and teacher conferences to talk about the first two books, I've had a number of interesting experiences that I'd like to share with you.

Often, adult women purchase *Girls to the Rescue* books and say, "I never had a book like this when I was growing up. So, please inscribe these books to me." We all need "stories to live by," so don't be surprised if your teacher, aunt, or grandma wants to borrow your book.

I am no longer surprised when boys buy a copy of *Girls to Rescue* and ask me to inscribe it to them. Nor am I surprised when boys tell me that they've read one of the stories from their sister's book and liked it so much they finished the whole book. I am thrilled that boys like these stories too. Loan your book to your brother. Don't be surprised if he enjoys it, too.

I hope you like this book of stories as well as the first two.

Happy reading.

Bruce Lansky

Hidden Courage

AN ORIGINAL STORY BY MARTHA JOHNSON

Kristin pulled the woolen shawl around her and hurried toward the barn. She'd been at Uncle Per's farm in Pennsylvania for three lonely weeks, and every day of this winter of 1890 had been colder than the last. Every day she felt more homesick for the crowded city apartment she and her father had shared. She missed her friends; she missed the warm smells of cooking that floated from every apartment; and most of all she missed Papa.

"It will just be a little time," Papa had promised, smoothing Kristin's blond braids. "You'll stay with Uncle Per until I find a farm for us." Papa's blue eyes had gotten a far-away look. "A farm like the one in Sweden."

That was always Papa's dream. Ever since he came to this new land, he'd talked about having a farm like the one he'd grown up on in Sweden. He talked about it so much that Kristin almost thought it was her dream too.

Until she came to Uncle Per's farm. She had been there three weeks, and after all that time she knew that she was never going to fit in on a farm. Deep inside, Kristin was very sad, thinking that Papa would be disappointed in her.

She didn't know how to do any of the things that Cousin Lars did, and he was only ten, a whole year younger than she was. What's more, she'd found out that she was afraid—afraid of everything about the farm, from the chickens who pecked at her when she gathered eggs to the bad-tempered sow in the pen by the barn.

Most of all, she was afraid of Thunder, the black mare. Thunder's huge hooves were big enough to squash Kristin, and Thunder tossed her head every time Kristin came near, as though she waited for a chance.

Kristin shoved the barn door open, checking to see if Lars lurked behind it. Ever since Lars realized she was afraid, he'd been teasing her. He jumped out of the loft at her yesterday, and the day before he chased her with what he said was a snake. It turned out to be an old empty snakeskin, but that was scary enough. Who knew what he'd think of next?

"Lars? Your father wants you," Kristin called. She looked around the echoing spaces of the barn. A few feeble rays of light filtered between the boards, making the shadows deeper. Thunder moved restlessly in her stall, and Kristin's heart started to thud. "I know you're in here, Lars. Did you hear me?"

"Boo!"

Kristin jumped as Lars pounced out of a stall.

"Kristin's a scaredy cat," Lars chanted, his round cheeks red with laughter.

"I am not!"

"Prove it," Lars said. "I dare you. I dare you to climb on Thunder's stall. I dare you."

Kristin clenched her hands into tight fists. "I'm not afraid."

Lars grinned. "Then do it. Climb on Thunder's stall. I double-dare you."

She wasn't going to turn down a double-dare. If she did, Lars would tease her about it for months. Kristin looked at the stall.

Thunder had moved to the far end, munching on

the hay Lars had just thrown down to her. Kristin could hop up to the top board and jump down again before Thunder came anywhere near her. That would show Lars.

Holding her breath, Kristin put one foot on the lowest board. Thunder didn't move. Quickly Kristin scrambled to the top, her heart pounding.

"See?" As fast as she said the word, Lars pushed her. Arms waving, Kristin lost her balance and tumbled into the stall with Thunder.

Sputtering, Kristin shook herself out of the hay. For a second she was so angry with Lars she forgot where she was. Then she looked up and found Thunder's face an inch from her own.

Kristin screamed. Thunder tossed her head, and her huge hooves danced dangerously near Kristin. Kristin was going to be trampled; she'd never get out…

"What's going on here?" Uncle Per's voice was the best sound Kristin had ever heard. His strong hands lifted her out of the stall. He set her on her feet and glared from her to Lars. "I asked a question. What happened? How did Kristin get in the stall?"

Lars looked down, his foot scuffing the dirt floor. "I…I guess I…I might have pushed her."

Uncle Per frowned. "Kristin, go into the house, please." He took hold of Lars' collar. "Lars and I will be in soon." Kristin didn't argue. She turned and ran toward the house as fast as she could go.

After supper, Uncle Per sat Kristin and Lars down at the kitchen table. Lars wiggled on his seat. "I do not like this fussing," Uncle Per said sternly. "Lars, no more teasing. Do you understand?"

"Yes, Papa," Lars muttered.

Uncle Per turned to her. "Kristin, I know the farm is strange to you. But you must try harder. Your papa wants you to learn while you are here."

Kristin nodded. Her heart was too full to say anything. She knew what Uncle Per meant. She was never going to be able to help Papa on the new farm. Lars was right. She was a scaredy cat.

The snow started the next morning, piling up quickly on the hemlocks and blurring the shapes of the outbuildings. At noon Uncle Per called Lars and Kristin.

"I want you to take the sleigh to town and pick up your mother," Uncle Per told Lars. "Take Kristin too."

"I don't need Kristin—" Lars began, but Uncle Per cut him off.

"The sleigh runs better with the extra weight," Uncle

Per said. His tone didn't leave room for argument.

Kristin bundled into her heaviest coat and tied her shawl around her head. When she got outside, Lars was hitching Thunder to the small sleigh. Its silvery runners would glide smoothly over the snow. Lars gave Kristin a look that said he'd rather do this by himself.

"Up you get." Uncle Per boosted her onto the seat and patted Thunder. "Be careful," he told Lars.

Lars frowned. "I know how to drive." He snapped the lines and clicked to Thunder, and the sleigh ran smoothly down the lane.

The breeze fluttered Kristin's shawl, and snowflakes danced in her face. Thunder's hoof beats were muffled by the thick white blanket of snow, and the runners glided so easily Kristin felt as though she were floating.

"This is so fast," she said before she remembered that it was Lars driving.

"You think this is fast?" Lars snapped the lines. "Look what Thunder can do."

Thunder obediently speeded up, and they raced through the snow. The wind stung Kristin's cheeks, and she grasped the side rail with one mittened hand. The snow was so thick she couldn't even tell where the road was.

"You're going too fast!" The wind took her words and blew them away.

Lars looked at her, his blue eyes laughing. He shouted something she couldn't make out and snapped the lines again. They whipped along the narrow road.

Kristin opened her mouth to protest as the sleigh swerved. The right runner dropped suddenly, as though the ground had fallen out from beneath it. The sleigh tipped. Kristin went flying, tumbling over and over through the snow to land, face down, in an icy drift.

For a moment she thought she'd never breathe again. Then she gasped in a mouthful of cold air mixed with snow. Kristin shoved herself upright, shaking snow from her hair and her eyes, and looked around.

Lars lay crumpled under the overturned sleigh. He clutched his left arm with his right hand and his face was whiter than the snow. Then Kristin saw Thunder, and her heart seemed to stop.

The frightened horse reared and whinnied. The reins tightened around Thunder's neck as her hooves pawed the air. If Thunder got much closer to Lars, she could trample him when her hooves came back down.

"Lars! Are you all right?" Kristin scrambled to her feet.

"My arm." Tears filled Lars' blue eyes. "I think it's broken." He choked back a sob as Thunder reared again. "Look at Thunder. We have to do something."

"Maybe someone will come…" Kristin began. Then she stopped. That was stupid. No one was going to come along this road in a snowstorm. And Lars could do nothing. It was up to her. "I'll do it."

As soon as the words were out of her mouth, Kristin wanted them back. What was she thinking? She was afraid even to get near the horse.

"You'll have to unhitch her and lead her free," Lars said. "If she jumps around, either she's going to get hurt or I will."

Kristin took a step toward Thunder, then another. Her feet didn't want to move, and her heart pounded so hard she could hear it. Thunder moved her hooves and tossed her head. Kristin stopped, panic sweeping over her. She couldn't do this—she just couldn't!

Suddenly she remembered herself standing on the railroad platform, waiting with Papa for the train to take her to Uncle Per's.

"Car three," Papa had said, looking at her ticket.

Kristin looked at the black railcars, lightly dusted with frost. They looked big and scary, and she couldn't imagine traveling in one of them all alone.

"I don't know which one," she said, and her voice choked with tears. "I don't know which one to get into."

Papa knelt until his face was level with hers. "It's not such a scary thing, Kristin." He reached out and wiped the frost from the side of the car. Underneath the layer of frost were green letters, appearing as though by magic. "You see? Car Three."

"I'm sorry," Kristin whispered. "I'm afraid."

Papa looked into her eyes, his face very close to hers. "I know," he said. His rough hand cradled her cheek. "But you are braver than you think, little Kristin. I know that you have courage here, inside." He touched her chest, above her heart.

She shook her head, ashamed to tell him he was wrong. She didn't have any courage.

He smiled. "Yes, it's there. It's just hiding." He nodded toward the letters on the train. "Like the letters were hidden under the frost. You can find it. When you need it, just wipe away the scared feeling. You'll find your courage, hidden underneath."

Her father's words seemed to echo in Kristin's head as she stood in the cold road, looking at Thunder. Courage, hidden courage. Papa believed she had it.

And Papa was never wrong.

Kristin took a deep breath, pushed the fear away, and bravely positioned herself between Thunder and Lars. Dodging to avoid Thunder's flying hooves, Kristin tried to grab the reins. But Thunder spooked and reared again. Kristin could see Lars' frightened face as he cringed under the sleigh. She had to keep trying.

On her third attempt, Kristin managed to grab the reins. With all of her strength, she tried to pull Thunder down and to steady her, calling out, "Whoa, girl! Whoa!" Finally she managed to get Thunder's front legs back on the ground.

The reins were coiled tightly around Thunder's neck. Kristin reached out and stroked the big horse's velvety neck, saying, "Steady, girl, steady." Thunder's eyes were wild with fear and she was breathing heavily and shaking. The huge horse was shaking with fear! Kristin realized that Thunder was even more afraid than she had been. At that thought, all of Kristin's fear disappeared.

Her fingers stiff and cold, Kristin unsnarled the tangled reins and unhooked the harness that trapped Thunder. The big horse snorted. Carefully, very carefully, Kristin led the trembling mare away from Lars and the overturned sleigh.

Kristin took a shaky breath. She'd done it. She looked up at Thunder's face, and the mare rubbed her nose against Kristin's coat.

"You did it," Lars said. "Good work, Kristin."

"Good work," Kristin repeated the words to herself. It *had* been good work. She tied Thunder to the nearest tree and hurried to tip the sleigh off Lars.

"Papa is going to be angry with me." Lars leaned against Kristin as she helped him sit up. "I'm sorry, Kristin, that I was so mean to you."

"It's all right." Kristin sat down next to him. Just like Thunder, Lars didn't seem scary any more.

Lars swallowed hard. "I guess I was jealous. Everybody was making a fuss about you. And you got to do so many things…live in the city, ride on the train…I've never been anywhere except on this stupid farm."

Kristin stared at him. "But Lars, you're the one who knows how to do everything. How to hitch up the horses and milk the cows; how to be a real help on the farm. Not like me."

"You could learn." Lars looked down at his arm. "I won't be much use for a while, but I can teach you."

She could learn. For the first time, that seemed possible to Kristin. She hugged her new-found courage. She could learn. When Papa sent for her, she'd be ready to be a real help on their own farm, the farm just like the one Papa left behind in Sweden.

Emily and the Underground Railroad

AN ORIGINAL STORY BY JOANNE MITCHELL

Emily handed the baby to Mrs. Harriman.

"Thank you, Emily. I don't know how I would manage without you," Mrs. Harriman said. She leaned back against her pillow, cuddling her baby against her. "You've been such a good worker these past few weeks while I've been getting my strength back."

Emily smiled. Helping Mrs. Harriman after her baby had been born was actually easier than being home, helping Ma with the six younger children. The best part was that she was actually getting paid for her work. Ma had promised that some of that pay would go for new dresses for Emily. Now that she was thirteen, she had grown so much that her ankles were showing and her old dresses had no more hem to let out. The rest of her pay would have to help buy shoes for the other children. Emily knew that her family needed the money.

As she picked up a basket and started to leave the room, Emily said, "I'll be back soon to put little Thomas back in his cradle. I'm going to gather eggs now."

"Check carefully for that little speckled hen's nest," Mrs. Harriman said. "She always likes to hide her eggs. Once I found her eggs in the apple-drying shed, and once in the barn."

"I'll look for her," Emily promised.

Outside the house Emily paused for a moment to admire the small apple orchard that spread to the north of the main house. The trees were in full bloom now, brilliantly white in the bright spring sunshine. The rest of Mr. Harriman's prosperous farm grew wheat, corn, and oats. Here in 1853 in western New York State, these were all important crops.

In the chicken coop, sure enough, the little speckled hen was not in sight. She always appeared promptly enough when Emily fed the chickens, so she couldn't be that far away. Emily checked quickly through the barn, but could find no sign of the hen. She pushed open the door of the apple-drying shed, unused at this season of the year. In the fall, farm workers sliced and dried apples from the orchard in this shed; the drying preserved the apples from spoiling. The bottom of the shed's door was broken, and the hen could have entered through the opening.

"Are you hiding your eggs in here, you rascally little hen?" she asked, talking to herself. Suddenly she thought she heard something—was that a rustling noise coming from behind those crates? As her eyes adjusted to the dim light, Emily stepped forward to look there and gasped.

Her heart thudded hard in her chest. She was looking straight into the eyes of a woman who was crouched down, trying to hide. The woman held her hand over the mouth of a small child she clutched to her side. The woman and child were black.

Escaped slaves! Emily's mind screamed at her. Escaped slaves hiding right in the apple-drying shed.

What should she do?

The woman's eyes held hers in silent pleading.

"Emily!" Mr. Harriman's voice called from right outside the shed, making Emily jump. "What are you doing in there?"

Emily made an instant decision about what she would do. She could never betray someone who needed her help the way these two people did. She called out, "I'm looking for the speckled hen's nest, Mr. Harriman. Mrs. Harriman said she had found it here once." Then she whispered to the slave, "Don't be afraid. I'll be back later."

The woman nodded. She looked less frightened.

Emily left the shed, carefully closing the door behind her. Mr. Harriman waited in front of the door. "I couldn't find the nest," she said. "Mrs. Harriman suggested the barn and the shed, but it wasn't there."

"Well, get along with your other work," Mr. Harriman said. "I don't pay you good money to lollygag around."

Emily returned to the house, mechanically going through her chores. She put little Thomas to bed and returned to the kitchen. As she sliced ham for frying, made cornbread, and baked an apple pie from last year's dried apples, Emily kept thinking about the slave and her little girl.

Emily knew that even though slavery had ended in most northern states such as New York, the Fugitive Slave Law had been passed three years ago, in 1850. The law said that slave hunters could come into the northern states to track down runaway slaves who had escaped from plantations in the South. The hunters could find the escaped slaves, handcuff them, and take them back to their owners. Emily also knew that anyone who returned a runaway slave received a big reward, while someone caught hiding or helping an escaped slave would be arrested and jailed. Just last month a male slave had been caught in nearby Rochester and taken in chains back to his owner in Tennessee. The man who had been hiding him was in jail.

To be free from capture, slaves had to go even farther north than New York; they had to go all the way to Canada. That meant crossing Lake Ontario by boat. Emily had heard whispers of a group called the Underground Railroad that helped escaped slaves reach Canada, but she knew no one who admitted to being part of it. How could anyone admit it, when openly belonging to that group could mean prison?

The Underground Railroad wasn't a real railroad, of course, as she'd first thought it was. It wasn't even underground. It was just a name for people who helped escaped slaves by passing them from one safe spot to another.

If only she could talk to Ma or Pa! But their house was seven miles away, too far to go to ask for advice. They had always said that slavery was unjust and wicked. She knew they would feel the way she did. What could she do to help the woman and her child?

After supper Mr. Harriman announced he was going to visit a neighbor. As his horse disappeared in the distance, Emily wrapped up a slice of ham, the leftover cornbread, some cheese, a slice of apple pie, and a small pitcher of milk. She crossed the yard to the shed, first looking carefully to make sure she was unseen.

"Hello?" Emily said softly into the darkness inside. "Are you still here? I've brought food."

A shadowy figure rose from the corner. "Bless you, child. We've not eaten for two days." The woman took the food eagerly, but made sure the youngster with her had eaten before she herself took a bite. "Oh, this is good."

Emily said, "My name is Emily. What's yours?"

"I'm Juno. And my daughter is Pandora. She's three. The master, he named us all from some old stories he knew."

Emily asked, "Where did you come from?"

"A plantation in Georgia. I had to leave. The master was going to sell my Pandora. I was a house slave, and he said he didn't want me wasting my time taking care of Pandora when I should be waiting on the mistress."

"Sell your baby away from you?" Emily was horrified. "Can he really do that?"

Juno laughed bitterly. "The master can do anything he wants. So I left; I had to. No one is taking my baby from me. My man ran away a year ago, after he was whipped. He always told me that if I got away I should follow the drinking gourd, and I did."

Emily was puzzled. "The drinking gourd?"

"You know, those stars that make the shape of a drinking gourd with a long handle. They show you the North Star, and you follow it to go north to freedom. To Canada." She said the last word slowly, like a prayer.

"Oh, I've always called it the Big Dipper. You came all the way from Georgia? On foot?" Emily had never been more than twenty-five miles from home. She had learned about Georgia in school. She couldn't imagine someone traveling all that distance on foot, carrying a small child with her.

"Part of the way we got to ride in a wagon, hidden under some burlap bags. Some people—they're called the Underground Railroad—help people like me. They pass us from one to another. I got through Pennsylvania that way. Last night I was supposed to get to another station, a safe house, but I lost my way in the dark. I ended up here on this farm as it was starting to get light. I thought we'd better hide before we were seen."

Emily was worried. "I don't know how to help you get away. I don't know where you could go to be safe. Lake Ontario is only five miles away, and Canada is on the other side, but I don't know who would take you across."

Juno said softly, "Emily, you've already helped us. I can't get you into trouble. We'll leave tonight and I'll try to find the right house by myself. It's supposed to be a house made of round stones. It has white shutters and a big oak tree in the front."

Emily wrinkled her forehead. A house made with round stones. That meant a cobblestone house, made from the fist-sized, round stones gathered from the lakeshore and laid in rows with mortar. "That might be Mr. Carpenter's house. That's the only one near here like that, white shutters and all. But he's supposed to be a mean old grouch. I can't believe that he would risk himself to help someone else."

"Tell me where it is and I'll try going there myself. I have no choice." Juno spoke with quiet dignity.

"No," Emily said. If Juno had the courage to come all this distance, then she, Emily, would find the courage to help. "I'll see Mr. Carpenter at church tomorrow. I'll find a way to ask him if he has a safe house. You stay here another day and I'll visit again tomorrow evening."

The next day Mr. Harriman took Emily and the hired hands to church in the wagon. Mrs. Harriman was still too weak to travel. On the way he lectured them all. "I heard last night that some escaped slaves might be in the area. A twenty-year-old woman and her young daughter. There is a reward out for their capture."

"I don't know about slavery," one of the men said. "Don't seem right, owning another person."

"The Bible mentions slaves," Mr. Harriman answered. "That makes it all right. They are valuable property and their owner deserves to get them back.

Besides, there's a federal law that says they have to be returned."

Emily made herself as inconspicuous as she could in the back of the wagon. She knew Juno would get no sympathy from Mr. Harriman.

After church service Emily spotted Mr. Carpenter checking his horse's harness. She sidled over to him, first making sure that Mr. Harriman was busy talking to someone else.

"Mr. Carpenter?" Emily said.

"Yes?" Mr. Carpenter said gruffly. He was old, with a short white beard and an unsmiling face. "Speak up, girl."

Emily's voice almost didn't work because her mouth was so dry. Her stomach rolled and for a moment she felt nauseated, because of the big risk she was taking. She considered leaving and letting Juno solve her own problems. After all, Emily hadn't asked to be involved. But no, she knew she could not abandon Juno, not after Juno had been so brave as to make it this far on her own. She could not let a young child be sold away from her mother.

"Mr. Carpenter," she said again, more firmly. "I am Emily Woodhall. I believe you know my parents,

David and Elizabeth Woodhall. I would like to ask you a question. Supposing, just supposing, that someone knew where an escaped slave might be hiding. How would that person go about finding a safe place to take that slave?"

Mr. Carpenter looked at her in silence. Emily guessed that he was wondering if he could trust her, the same way she was wondering if she could trust him. Each of them would be able to have the other arrested and jailed.

"Well, now, Emily, you have an honest face. I know your parents and they are good people. Would this supposed slave that your supposed someone found be a woman with a child?"

"Yes, sir," she said.

"Good. I have been worried about them. Can you bring them to my house? Tonight?" At her nod he said, "I'll expect you. Back door." He walked away swiftly.

That night Emily waited until Mr. and Mrs. Harriman had been in bed for what seemed like a long time. She tiptoed down the stairs to the back door, holding her shoes in her hand and remembering to avoid the squeaky step. She quietly slipped out into the night with the bag of food she had prepared earlier.

"Juno?" she whispered into the shed. "Are you here?"

"Yes, Emily. I was about getting ready to leave this place. My Pandora is tired of keeping quiet and I was afraid we'd get caught."

While Juno and Pandora ate hungrily, Emily explained what had happened. They were going to have to walk about four miles to Mr. Carpenter's house. Fortunately, a half moon was out, which would give them some light. It would be too risky to take a lantern.

They stumbled along the road, which had deep ruts from wagon traffic. Emily slipped into the mud puddles that were all too common on the road. Her leather boots became soaked and muddy, but she knew that Juno's shoes were cracked and worn out. Juno was also carrying Pandora. If Juno could walk without complaining, then so could Emily.

If someone came along, they were prepared to jump into the roadside bushes and lie flat. They knew they would hear a horse from a long way off. Fortunately, no one was out traveling in the dark.

Finally they came to Mr. Carpenter's house. They circled around to the back. There was no sign that anyone was awake. Emily knocked timidly at the back door. It opened suddenly, showing Mr. Carpenter holding a candle.

"Come in, come in," he urged, ushering them down a hall and into the sitting room. "Here," he said, handing the candle to Emily. He dragged the settee to the side of the room and kicked the rug out of the way. There, previously hidden under the rug, was a metal ring set into the wooden floor. Mr. Carpenter pulled up on the ring and a trap door opened, revealing a ladder down to a small basement room.

"Down there," he pointed. "There's a mat where you can sleep, and extra candles and flint. I have a boat to Canada arranged for tomorrow. Quickly! We must have you safely hidden."

Juno took a step forward. She stopped and looked at Emily. "I'll never forget you, child. I'll pray for you forever."

Emily's eyes filled with tears. "Oh, Juno!" She threw her arms around Juno and Pandora and gave them both a big hug. "I'll remember you the rest of my life."

On the way back to the Harrimans' house, Emily was tired but jubilant. She had done it! Even though she had been afraid, she had done it.

Emily managed to slip back into the house without being heard. Morning came before she was ready to get out of bed. She got through her chores that day almost by sleepwalking. Were Juno and Pandora safe, she wondered. Had the boat come? Had they reached Canada? Would she ever know?

The next week after church, Mr. Carpenter winked at Emily. "That 'package' you gave me got delivered safely," he said quietly. "The best part is that she found her husband. Thanks to you, they are a family again."

"And thanks to you," Emily said. She knew better than to ask how many other fugitives had found shelter under Mr. Carpenter's sitting room floor. "If you need help again, call on me."

What had she said? Emily couldn't believe what had just come out of her mouth. After all the worry and fear, she had just volunteered to do it again. But as she thought about it, she knew it was true. Nothing in her life had ever felt as good as knowing that she had helped rescue two lives. And she would do it again and again if she had the chance.

"Good-bye, Juno," she whispered. "I'll never forget you."

Sarah's Pickle Jar

ADAPTED BY BRUCE LANSKY
FROM A CHINESE FOLKTALE

Polish Word:

Zloty (pronounced "ZLO-tee"): Polish money. One American dollar is equal to about three zlotys.

Yiddish Words:

Oy gevalt (pronounced "oee ge-VALT"): means "Oh, my goodness."

On Monday business was very slow for Izzy the Tailor. He worked in the back room of a clothing shop in Chelm, a village in Poland too small to appear on any map. Not a single customer had come in all day, so by four o'clock Izzy decided to leave work early.

After all, what is the point of staying at work if there's nothing to do?

As he walked through town, Izzy lingered at a bakery window. He wanted to buy some pastries, but he hadn't made a single zloty all day.

Izzy was hungry, and the sight of so many good things to eat led him into the bakery. He stood in front of the glass counter, which was filled with apple strudels, poppy-seed cakes, and cheese Danishes that, believe me, are to die for.

As he gazed at the pastries, Izzy took a deep breath and sighed. A smile replaced the sad expression that had been on his face. The smell of the pastries was so divine, Izzy thought for a moment that he had died and gone to heaven.

"Good afternoon, Izzy," said Jacob the Baker. "What can I do for you? A piece of fresh-baked apple strudel, perhaps?"

"Just looking," said Izzy.

Now business had been slow at the bakery too, and Jacob had a lot of unsold pastries that were growing staler by the hour. So his mood had grown increasingly sour as the day went on.

"Just looking, my foot!" said the frustrated baker.

"You're also smelling. And smelling will cost you a zloty."

Izzy looked at the baker incredulously. "You must be kidding!"

"You are standing in my bakery, filling up your nose with the smell of my pastries. Pay me the zloty and be on your way."

"I'm sorry, but I don't have a zloty in my pocket. If I did, I would have bought a piece of strudel," Izzy explained.

"Whether you fill up on the smell of strudel or the taste of strudel, it's all the same to me. I'll see you in court tomorrow morning!" the baker barked.

When Izzy got home he did not greet his wife, Rivka, with a kiss as he usually did. He did not greet his daughter, Sarah, with a hug as he usually did. Instead, he slumped in his armchair and stared into space.

"What happened to my kiss?" asked Rivka.

"What happened to my hug?" asked Sarah.

Izzy groaned, "Did I have a bad day?" Although it sounded like a question, Rivka and Sarah knew that it was the answer.

"Tell me what happened," asked Sarah.

"You don't want to know," replied Izzy, rolling his eyes. Then he told his sad story.

"*Oy gevalt!*" Do you have problems!" exclaimed Rivka.

"Don't worry, Father. I'll think of something," said Sarah. She put her arms around his neck and gave him a hug. Then she went off to bed.

The next morning Sarah refused to go to school. Over her mother's objections, she went to court with Izzy. Eyes downcast, Izzy shuffled along slowly, trying to delay the inevitable. Sarah eagerly pulled her father forward with one hand, while clutching a small, glass pickle jar with the other.

Now I must tell you that the court in Chelm was in session only when the occasion arose. The location varied, depending on what day of the week it was. Since it was Tuesday, the courtroom was at Herschel the Banker's office, which explains why Herschel the Banker was the presiding judge. But word of the case had spread, and Herschel's office was overflowing with curious onlookers.

"The court will come to order," announced Herschel, while banging his coffee mug on his desk like a gavel. "Jacob, present your case."

The baker told the court what had happened the day before and ended with this claim: "He filled his nose with the smell of my pastries then stood there drooling with an idiotic grin on his face."

"Izzy, what do you have to say for yourself?" the banker asked.

"I was hungry, Your Honor, and was so overcome by the aroma of the pastries that I just stood there and enjoyed the smell. I beg for mercy. I am just a poor tailor with a family to support."

Herschel then tapped on his coffee mug with his spoon. "It's an open and shut case. You filled your nose with the smell of Jacob the Baker's pastries. The court finds you guilty as charged and orders you to pay the fine of one zloty."

Jacob the Baker smiled broadly as friends congratulated him on his court victory. Merchants lined up to shake Herschel the Banker's hand and pat him on the back. "A wise decision," they said.

Izzy, dejected, stepped forward to pay the fine. But Sarah grabbed his hand, pulling him back. "Excuse me, Your Honor. I have come to pay my father's fine with money I've saved in this pickle jar." She held up a glass jar full of coins. The room was suddenly quiet as all eyes turned to the girl.

Then Sarah shook the pickle jar. The sound of coins

jingling filled the room. "Your Honor, I wonder if the baker can hear the zlotys jingling in my pickle jar?"

"Of course I can hear them," Jacob the Baker snapped gruffly.

"Good. My father filled his nose with the smell of your pastries and now you have filled your ears with the sound of my money." Then, turning to the judge, she said, "Your Honor, the fine has been paid."

The courtroom buzzed as Herschel the Banker banged his coffee mug on the desk and announced, "Paid in full. Case closed!"

Izzy picked up Sarah and hugged her tightly. "This is the hug I forgot to give you when I came home last night."

Bai and the Tree of Life

An Original Story by Anne Schraff

A rice farmer and his wife lived in the Philippines, with five sons and one daughter. The daughter's name was Bai and she worked hard alongside her brothers in the terraced rice fields. Bai's mother wove baskets from coconut tree leaves and every month the family went to town to sell the baskets.

"Bai," Father said one day, "we are lucky to have the coconut trees. They are the tree of life. Look at the beautiful baskets your mother weaves. Soon you will weave them too."

"I don't want to weave baskets," Bai declared.

"But you must," Father said, shocked. "All the girls and the women weave baskets."

"We already have too many baskets," Bai said. She sat under the coconut tree and thoughtfully twirled the coconut leaves in her hands.

Bai's eldest brother watched her. "What are you doing, little sister?" he asked, smiling.

Bai's fingers worked quickly as she wove the coconut leaves. "I am making a hat," Bai said.

Bai's brother laughed heartily. "A hat? You are wasting good coconut leaves on a silly hat?" he exclaimed.

Bai's five brothers gathered to make fun of Bai.

"She is too lazy to help Mother weave baskets but she has time to make foolish hats," one of the brothers said.

"Bai is the silliest girl in the village," Bai's eldest brother complained.

Bai ignored her brothers as her fingers guided the leaves into the shape of a hat.

The next day, after Bai was finished working in the rice fields, she went off by herself to finish the hat. Then she made another hat, even more quickly than before. She held the hat up, twirled it, and smiled at how cleverly made it was. Her heart raced with excitement.

That evening Bai made more hats, working in the twilight until the sun had gone down.

"Where is Bai?" Father asked.

Bai's brothers laughed bitterly. "She is playing somewhere," said one brother.

"She is lazy," another brother said.

Father frowned. He went outside to find Bai finishing a hat. "Bai, you waste time playing. You are a young woman and should help your mother weave baskets."

Bai smiled at her father and held up one of her newly made hats. "Look, Father," she said, "this hat will protect whoever wears it from the hot midday sun."

"It's a nice hat, daughter," Bai's father admitted, "but it's not a basket."

But every day after she finished working in the rice fields, Bai continued to make more hats. And still more hats. Sometimes she wove into the crown of the hat a colorful parrot feather. Sometimes she interwove colored threads with the leaves to make a hat especially beautiful. She also dyed braided coconut husks and wove them into the hats in many bright colors, so each hat stood out a little from the others.

Father peered from the window in the evening and watched the small, intent figure of his daughter working on the hats. She had a stack of them done; each fit neatly into the next, so they could be easily carried. "What will become of her?" Bai's father groaned.

Mother shook her head too, but for a different reason. "Leave the child alone," she said. When Mother was young, she had dreams too. People laughed at her dreams, so she forgot them. As a girl Bai's age, Mother had wanted to carve coconut shells into animal faces instead of household utensils as everyone else did. Now she worked hard and made baskets that often did not sell well. She was sorry she had packed up her dreams and sent them away so quickly.

On the next market day, the whole family waited for the large open ferryboat that would take them to town. Mother carried some baskets she had made, and her sons carried more. Mother had woven many, many baskets from coconut leaves.

Bai carried a huge stack of hats. As the sun became hotter, she chose from her stack a pretty hat with a blue parrot feather and gave it to her mother. "The sun will be even hotter in the market, Mother. This hat will help," Bai said.

Mother put the hat on and smiled. Her long, black hair streamed down from under the wide hat. "It makes me cooler already," she declared.

"And you look pretty, Mother," Bai said.

Father touched his head and felt the heat bear down. Perhaps a hat would not be such a bad idea. "Give me a hat, Bai. At least what you did should be put to some use," he said.

Bai gave her father a hat decorated with black thread and said, "You look very handsome in the hat, Father."

Bai's brothers also claimed hats, and they had to admit they helped in the hot sun. Besides, they were wonderfully made, woven skillfully without a flaw. Even though they didn't say so, they thought that Bai was very clever at this hat-making.

Mother watched as other families unloaded their baskets from the ferryboat and headed for the market-place. She hoped that somehow her baskets would stand out as sturdier or more attractive.

The family found a spot in the crowded market-place and they set up a table. Mother arranged all her baskets. Then she smiled and winked at Bai. She left a corner of the table empty for Bai's hats.

Soon people began to gather at the table, but they all crowded around Bai's hats.

"I will buy the yellow one," a pretty girl said, putting down her money and happily placing the hat on her head. The girl's brothers bought hats too, choosing ones trimmed in red. Only one of Mother's baskets sold, but soon Bai's stack of hats had vanished and still people wanted to buy.

Since the sun was going down and the family would soon be going home, they had no need of their own hats. So they all sold the hats from their heads.

Father's money sack was heavy as they boarded the ferryboat for the journey home.

"Bai," Mother said, "you must show me how to weave your wonderful hats."

"I will," Bai said. "You make such beautiful baskets, you'll make beautiful hats too."

Bai's brothers were very quiet on the way down the river to their village. Father counted the money again and a joyous smile touched his face. "My sons," he said, "I see no reason why boys cannot weave hats too, if their clever sister patiently teaches them."

Bai's mother laughed and Bai giggled softly. Even Bai's five brothers finally smiled and nodded. And though they could never weave hats as beautifully as Bai, they were very good at finding fallen parrot feathers and braiding dyed coconut husks for trim.

Young Maid Marian and Her Amazing, Astounding Pig

AN ORIGINAL STORY BY STEPHEN MOOSER

The Sheriff of Nottingham, a cruel and greedy man, once ruled Sherwood Forest. The Sheriff, who had cold blue eyes and a beard cut sharp as the letter V, had been taxing his subjects so harshly that many of them were now on the verge of losing everything they owned. All across the forest, families were struggling to keep their homes, save their lands, and simply stay alive.

However, even in the worst of times, rays of light do shine through. Sherwood Forest also had such a ray, and her name was Maid Marian. Although she was barely thirteen, her quick wit and wild pranks delighted her many friends and filled her father's home with laughter and love.

One sunny day, when Marian was outside chasing a piglet about the yard, a neighbor, Thomas the Woodsman, came down the road, his shoulders bent beneath the weight of a huge ax.

"Thomas! How are you today?" cried Marian.

Thomas raised up his head and gave Marian a sad, soulful look that described his feelings at that moment.

Thinking that Thomas needed to be cheered up, Marian scooped up the little pig in her arms and skipped across the yard, with her long hair flapping behind her like a golden blanket in the wind.

"Where are you going, my friend?" she asked.

Thomas paused at the gate and regarded Marian sadly with eyes as dark as his tangled beard.

"Have you not heard the terrible news?" he said. "The Sheriff's men are coming to collect yet another tax. If I don't give them half of my wood in payment, they'll take away my cottage and leave my family homeless."

Marian furrowed her brow. "But without that wood, how will you heat your home this winter? And what will you have to sell?"

"That I do not know," said Thomas. He shuffled his feet in the dust and drew in a deep breath. "Without a fire, my family and I could freeze. And without the money I'd make from selling the wood, we can't buy food."

"Ai-yeee!" The piglet in Marian's arms let out a sudden squeal. "Aiyee! Aiyee!"

Marian smiled. "Timothy said that the Sheriff should mind his own business and quit taxing us to death."

Thomas returned Marian's smile. "You have a very wise pig," he said. "How did you ever teach him to talk?"

Marian rubbed her knuckles along the pig's back and he squealed again. "Aiyee! Aiyee!" screeched Timothy.

"Getting him to talk is easy," she said. "Understanding what he says is the hard part."

"You're a very funny girl," said Thomas. He gave Marian a pat on the shoulder. "You and your pig have made me smile for the first time all day." He paused for a moment and looked wistfully off into the distance. "If only your pig really could talk. Perhaps he'd be able to tell me how to save my wood."

"Perhaps he could," said Marian. She narrowed her eyes and put her clever mind into action. "Now, when exactly did you say the tax collectors are coming?"

"The day after tomorrow," said Thomas. "I'm sure they will stop here as well."

"No doubt they will," said Marian. "The Sheriff has been trying for years to drive my father, Geoffrey the Magistrate, and me from our estate. He wants to take every last gold coin from our pockets."

"Your father has been a fair judge to us all," said Thomas. "I hope the Sheriff never succeeds in driving you from your home."

Marian rubbed her chin and thought. A plan had begun bubbling away in her head, like water in a teakettle. "You know what?" she said. "Maybe my piglet really can save us."

"This is no time for jokes," said Thomas. He wiped his nose with a ragged sleeve. "In two days my family could be in terrible trouble. Perhaps yours will be too."

"Not if Timothy has anything to say about it," said Marian. She rubbed the pig's back and he let out a long, piercing squeal. "In fact, he just predicted that the Sheriff's men won't get your wood or my father's gold."

Thomas eyed Marian as if she'd suddenly slipped her senses. "Please, Marian, I told you I'm in no mood for joking."

"The Sheriff's tax collectors may be strong, but they are not very smart," said Marian. "Trust me. I have a feeling everything is going to be fine."

Thomas shook his head, waved good-bye half-heartedly, and shuffled off down the road.

"Stop worrying!" shouted Marian as he walked slowly away, still shaking his head. "Timothy will come to the rescue!"

Thomas raised a hand in farewell but didn't turn around. A few minutes later the woodsman, bent beneath the weight of his giant ax, crested a small hill and was gone.

Marian worked on her plan all the rest of the day. The next morning she hurried to the large stone house of her best friend, a boy named Robin.

"Robin!" she cried, pounding on the heavy wooden door. "I need your help!"

A few minutes later the door swung open and a tall, sandy-haired boy, thin as a wick, came outside rubbing his eyes.

"Good heavens, Marian, do you know what hour it

is?" he said, shading his eyes against the morning sun. "I was sound asleep."

"We have no time to waste," said Marian. "I've got a plan and I need your help to carry it out."

Robin rolled his eyes skyward. "Please, not another one of your plans." He shook his head. "Your last scheme nearly cost us our lives. Remember when we snuck into the Sheriff's ball and filled our pockets with fruit for our hungry neighbors?"

"And we succeeded too," said Marian.

"Just barely," said Robin. "I was so weighted down with apples and pears that the Sheriff's soldiers nearly caught me running away."

Marian looked around and lowered her voice. "We have to work fast. The tax collectors are coming tomorrow."

"I know," said Robin, nodding. "My father says that if we don't give the Sheriff half of our money, he may try to claim part of our estate."

"If my plan works, he'll have nothing to fear," said Marian. She put a hand on her friend's shoulder. "Can I count on you to help?"

"Help? What kind of help?" asked Robin cautiously.

"I just need you to spread the word about Timothy."

"Timothy? Who's he?"

"My talking pig," said Marian. "He predicts the future too. Sort of."

Robin laughed. "Is this a joke? Pigs don't talk."

Marian tapped her friend on the nose. "I'll explain everything later. Please, I can't do this all by myself." When Robin hesitated, Marian raised two fingers and held them out. "Two forever?"

Robin sighed. "All right, two forever," he said, touching Marian's fingers with the tips of his own.

Two forever. It was a ritual the pair had performed many times. Two forever. That was the deal. When one asked for help, the other always had to agree, quickly and without complaint.

Tax collecting day dawned bright and sunny, but as the Sheriff's tax collectors, Simon and Norman, set out from town in their cart, dark clouds began sweeping in from the west, threatening rain.

At each house along the road, no matter how grand or how humble, Simon and Norman drew up to the door and called the owners to come out.

"By the order of the Sheriff of Nottingham, bring out your taxes and place them in the cart!" cried Simon, who was wearing a tight leather cap ringed by silver spikes.

"Be quick about it or you'll find yourself in the castle dungeon and your home in ashes!" added Norman, who lacked both hair on his head and brains within.

"Here are some of my most valuable possessions," said Christopher the Hunter, carefully placing some of his finest arrows in the back of the cart. "However, I doubt if you will deliver these to the Sheriff. Timothy told me this will be a very unlucky day for you both."

Norman raised his bushy eyebrows. "Timothy? Who is this Timothy?"

"Why, Timothy the Pig, of course. He predicts the future. And quite accurately too. Two days ago he said you would come at precisely this hour, and sure enough, here you are," Christopher said, repeating to the tax collectors the very words Marian had instructed him to say.

"Nonsense," snorted Simon. He snapped the reins and the cart lurched off down the road. "I've never heard such a ridiculous thing. Imagine, a pig that can predict the future."

At each house the story was the same. "Here is my bag of gold," said Mary the Merchant, placing the heavy sack in the back of the cart. "And, Simon, I see you are wearing the hat Timothy predicted you would wear. I'm sure you'd agree he's a very amazing pig."

Simon took off his hat and examined it. "Really? He said I would wear this?"

"With silver spikes around the bottom," Mary said, describing the hat just as she saw it at that moment.

Simon shook his head. "Incredible. I think I'd like to meet this pig."

At the next home, Anne the Seamstress placed a fine velvet cloak with a fur trim into the cart. She looked up at the darkening sky. Any fool could see that rain was coming. "Hurry up. I don't want this cloak to get wet before it gets to the Sheriff. Timothy predicted a storm."

Norman sniffed the air. "I think he's right again," he said. "A storm is coming. Do you think this amazing pig might be able to predict my own future?"

"Of course," said Mary, repeating the words Robin had told her to say. "Anyone can ask him anything."

When the tax collectors stopped at the next home, Thomas the Woodsman quickly appeared, holding an armload of his precious wood. "You can come back for the rest later," he said, placing it into the cart. "Timothy told me that by winter I'd have more wood than I need."

By now the Sheriff's tax collectors could no longer contain their curiosity.

"Tell us, Thomas, where can we find this astounding pig?" asked Simon.

"You'll find him at your very last stop, the home of Maid Marian," said Thomas. He glanced up at the thick clouds. "Hurry now. It's about to rain."

And so, spurred on by the threat of rain and the promise that they'd soon meet Timothy, the astounding pig, the tax collectors hurried to Marian's house.

When they arrived, they found Marian outside with the piglet in her arms and her father by her side. But they did not see Robin hiding behind a nearby tree.

"I have the Sheriff's tax money," said Marian's father, Geoffrey the Magistrate. He showed Norman and Simon the coins inside a leather bag. "I'll place it in the back of the cart."

"Do that and be quick about it," ordered Simon. "We must get back before the clouds burst."

"And they soon will," said Marian, for she had already felt a drop. "My pig has predicted a downpour."

Norman raised an eyebrow. "What else has your pig predicted?" he asked, trying not to seem too curious. "Could he tell me my own future, for instance?"

Marian rubbed Timothy's back and the pig went, "Aiyeee!" "He says he knows everything about your future," said Marian.

Norman leaned forward eagerly and so did Simon. "Tell us, little pig, will we find happiness and riches?"

"Perhaps," said Marian, approaching the cart. "Listen carefully to what Timothy has to say." For the next few minutes Marian rubbed Timothy's back, and each time he squealed, she made up something about Simon's and Norman's futures.

All this time, while Simon and Norman greedily followed Marian's words and Timothy's squeals, Robin was removing the goods and gold from the back of the cart. As he took away each item, he substituted it with something else. The bags of gold and coins he replaced with sacks of rocks, the arrows he exchanged for sticks, the wood he traded for twigs, and in place of Anne's fine cloak he put a rag. When he was done, he signaled to Marian and returned to his hiding place behind the tree.

"Timothy has one final prediction," said Marian. She rubbed her pig's back and he squealed long and loud. "Sadly, he says this will be an unlucky day for you both. In fact, the Sheriff is going to be so displeased with the two of you that he may very well take away your jobs."

"Nonsense," said Simon, shaking his head.

"Flumadiddle!" said Norman. "We are the best tax collectors the Sheriff has ever had."

Marian shrugged her shoulders. "I am only reporting the pig's words," she said. "And he says the Sheriff will not be happy with the worthless things you have collected."

"Now I know your pig doesn't know what he's talking about," said Simon. "Our cart is loaded with all the riches in the land."

Just then, before anyone, including Timothy, could say another word, the clouds split open and the rain began to pour down as though a dam had burst.

"Hurry!" urged Marian. "The road will soon be awash in mud."

"We're on our way!" exclaimed Simon. He snapped the reins and the cart rattled away toward the Sheriff's castle.

Although it rained long and hard, Norman and Simon eventually pulled through the castle gates. As they clattered to a halt in the courtyard, the Sheriff came out to claim his precious taxes.

"What have you brought me?" he asked, stroking

his pointed beard. "Show me what you have collected."

"See for yourself," said Norman, who, like Simon, was dripping like a wet rag. "The treasure is all in the back of the cart."

When the Sheriff stuck his head into the back of the cart, he didn't see an ounce of treasure anywhere.

"What is this? Some kind of a joke?" he said, emptying the rocks from a bag. "Don't you know the difference between a stone and a nugget of gold?"

"But...but, sir," blubbered Simon. "I assure you we—"

"And what do you call this?" thundered the Sheriff, holding up the rag.

"A cloak for you?" suggested Norman, wincing. "I don't remember it looking like that when—"

"And what are these!" bellowed the Sheriff, casting the sticks and twigs onto the ground. "You call this treasure? Do you take me for a fool!"

Simon and Norman looked at each other and gasped. "It's just as Timothy the Pig predicted!" exclaimed Simon. "The things we collected are worthless."

"You're fired, both of you!" shouted the Sheriff. He threw up his arms in exasperation. "I've never known such cabbage-headed idiots."

All Norman and Simon could do was shake their heads in wonder. "Amazing," said Norman. "The pig predicted we'd lose our jobs. And we did. Incredible!"

"I don't know what you two are talking about, but I want you out of my sight forever!"

Before the Sheriff could change his mind and throw them into the dungeon, Norman and Simon hopped off the cart and raced away into the countryside.

"And never come back!" yelled the Sheriff, shaking his fist at the fleeing men. He kicked at the worthless pile of goods at his feet. Ka-blam! His foot rammed right into one of the stones. "Ouch! Ow! Ow!" he roared, hopping up and down on his foot.

As the Sheriff spent the next week in bed, nursing his broken toes, the people of Sherwood Forest retold the story of how Marian and Robin had fooled the tax collectors and saved their precious goods. Everyone agreed that Maid Marian had to be the cleverest soul in all of Sherwood Forest.

But then, even a pig could have told you that.

Dear Reader: If you enjoyed this story, you will also like the novel based on this story: *Young Marian's Adventures in Sherwood Forest.* Look for it in your bookstore starting September 1997.

Kamala and the Thieves

ADAPTED BY BRUCE LANSKY
FROM AN INDIAN FOLKTALE

Indian Words:

Rupee (pronounced "ROO-pee"): Indian money. One
American dollar is equal to about thirty-five rupees.

Rajah (pronounced "RA-zha"): a title for an Indian ruler or
prince.

If you were a girl raised in a poor village in Punjab,
India, you would probably be married off by your
well-meaning parents to a young man with good
prospects. That's the way it was when Kamala was

growing up some years ago. So that is why Kamala's parents arranged a marriage with Rajiv, the barber's son.

Kamala complained to her parents. "Who is this Rajiv? How can you marry me to someone I've never even met before?"

"Don't worry," Kamala's mother assured her. "Rajiv is a fine boy from a hard-working family. His father owns the busiest barber shop in the village. Rajiv will work there when he gets out of school. He'll take good care of you, and you'll be very happy together. You'll see." And so Kamala's mother proceeded to make arrangements for the marriage.

One day after school, Kamala walked home past the barber shop. It was a hot day, and the door was open. She glanced around the shop and caught a glimpse of Rajiv chatting with a customer. That was the only time she ever saw Rajiv—until, of course, the day of the wedding. But by then it was too late.

Kamala didn't find out until after she was married that Rajiv spent all day at the barber shop joking and playing cards with his friends, not cutting hair. And what little money he made, Rajiv lost at the card table.

Although Kamala kept her home spotless and did

what she could to scrimp and save, sometimes Rajiv did not bring home enough money for food. To make ends meet, Kamala did odd jobs for neighbors. She took care of young children and cooked while their mothers carried their laundry down to the river and washed it. Kamala also watched over their belongings to keep them safe from thieves who prowled the neighborhood.

One day Rajiv came home without a rupee in his pocket. "Don't worry, Kamala. I have a plan to get rich. The Rajah's son is getting married and everyone in the village is invited. I will go to the feast and perhaps the Rajah will grant me a favor."

"I hope your plan works, Rajiv. But if it doesn't, I've decided to get a job. You can take care of the cleaning and cooking."

Rajiv protested, but he knew that Kamala was right. So he staked all his hopes on the Rajah. If Kamala took a job, everyone would know that he could not support his family.

At the wedding reception there was a long line of well-wishers, and tables filled with sumptuous food. Rajiv had never seen so much food, so he stuffed himself instead of waiting in line to speak to the Rajah. By the time Rajiv had finished eating, the reception was almost over.

Rajiv approached the Rajah. "Your Excellency," said Rajiv as he bowed, "permit me to congratulate you on this happy occasion."

"Thank you for your kind words," answered the Rajah. "And now, if you'll excuse me, I was just preparing to retire."

Rajiv had not come to the wedding just to flatter the Rajah. He had come to ask for a favor. If he did not speak up, he would have to go home empty-handed.

Rajiv bowed again. "Your Excellency, I am just a poor barber. I wonder if you'd be so kind as to grant me a small favor on this happy occasion."

A frown creased the brow of the Rajah. He did not know this young man and had no reason to grant him a favor. But to avoid creating an unpleasant scene at the wedding reception, he said, "They say it is bad luck to refuse a request at a wedding, so I will grant you a favor.

"I own some land at the edge of town that is not being cultivated. If you plant it, I will let you keep half of the money you make."

Rajiv bowed low. "Thank you, Excellency, for your generosity." But as he walked home, he was not smiling. Rajiv had been hoping for a few rupees, not a plot of land to farm. Farming was hard work.

When Kamala saw the expression on his face, she sensed the news was bad. "What happened?" she asked. "Didn't the Rajah grant you a favor?"

"I shouldn't have wasted my time," answered Rajiv. "The Rajah was very stingy. He gave me some land to farm for a share of the profits."

"Why are you complaining?" asked Kamala. "Your plan has succeeded!"

"You must be crazy!" snapped Rajiv. "How can I farm without a plow or a bull to pull it?"

"Leave that to me," answered Kamala. "You take care of the cooking and cleaning. I'll take care of the farming."

That day Kamala went out to look at the Rajah's land. It was full of weeds. The soil was good, but hard—it had not been plowed for years. "Maybe Rajiv was right. How will I plow this land?" Kamala wondered. She thought of nothing else all night. The next day she had an idea.

Kamala set out for the land with three children she had in her care. They all carried sticks she had sharpened. As soon as they arrived at the Rajah's land, they began walking around the land, poking their sticks into the ground. People passing by stopped to gape at this strange sight. As a crowd gathered, it attracted some thieves looking for pockets to pick.

When Kamala and the children began to walk back to the village, a thief named Mustapha approached and asked, "Why were you poking the ground with sticks?"

She responded, "It is a secret. I will tell you only if you promise not to tell a soul."

"I promise," said the thief solemnly.

"My husband, Rajiv, was at the Rajah's wedding feast yesterday. The Rajah told him that gold is hidden in this land. I am looking for it."

That night while the village slept, Mustapha and his gang of thieves arrived at the Rajah's land with shovels. They dug up every foot of land looking for the hidden gold. The next morning they were tired and angry at not finding a single coin.

When they saw Kamala approaching, they hid in the forest near the land. They watched as she began to plant seeds in the newly "plowed" soil.

Mustapha left his hiding place and confronted her. "You lied when you said that gold is hidden in the land."

"I didn't lie. There is gold hidden in this land, but to find it, you must plant crops and harvest them." Then, spying several other thieves hiding in the forest, she said, "I see that you lied when you promised you would keep my secret."

Every day Kamala weeded and watered her crop. It was hard work. And when she got home, Rajiv had dinner cooked and ready for her. At the end of the summer, Rajiv helped Kamala harvest the crop and take it to market.

She gave Rajiv half the gold to take to the Rajah, and buried the rest under an apple tree that grew outside her kitchen. She covered the hole with leaves, and leaned a ladder against the tree to make it look as though she had been picking apples. Unfortunately, Rajiv stopped at the barber shop and bragged to his friends about all the gold he had made farming the Rajah's land.

Word quickly got out to Mustapha, who stopped Kamala on the way to the market. "Now that you have found the gold that was hidden in the land, I have come for my share. After all, I dug up the field for you and should be paid for my labor."

Kamala replied, "You dug up the field only because

you wanted to steal the gold that was hidden there. I will not pay you a rupee."

But Mustapha did not give up. When Kamala returned from the market, she saw him hiding behind the tree. And when Rajiv returned from delivering the gold to the Rajah that night, he noticed someone lurking in the shadows.

"I hope you have hidden the gold well, Kamala," said Rajiv. "Otherwise the thieves will surely steal it and we will be no better off than we were before."

"Don't worry, Rajiv," Kamala said in a voice loud enough to be heard through the open window. "I have hidden the gold in the tree, where no one would think of looking for it."

Mustapha overheard Kamala and looked up. High in the apple tree, hidden behind dense leaves and fruit, he saw something that looked like a sack. He ran to his hideout and returned shortly with three of his gang.

"Hold the ladder while I go up to get the gold," he commanded. "And be ready when I cut it down." Two men grabbed the ladder, while another stood under the sack, ready to catch it.

Mustapha scampered up the ladder and then from branch to branch until he was close enough to the sack to cut it down with his knife. Not finding any rope, he cut a branch off the tree and hit the sack with it to knock it down.

The sack stayed put, and so Mustapha poked it and heard a buzzing sound. He hit it harder and the buzzing sound got louder. He hit it as hard as he could and knocked it down. And as it fell, angry hornets buzzed out of their nest and swarmed over Mustapha. He started screaming.

"Keep quiet! You'll wake up the neighbors," called the thief who was trying to catch the nest. But in an instant, he heard the buzzing sound and felt the stings of the angry hornets. "Run!" he cried out to the two thieves who were holding the ladder.

But they didn't need any urging. The angry hornets had found them too. Frantically climbing down the tree with one hand while trying to beat the hornets away with the other, Mustapha put his foot on the ladder, knocking it over—no one was holding it. He had no choice but to jump. He landed on his foot, which buckled under his weight. Then he hopped after his men who had jumped into the river to elude the stinging hornets.

"Now we're rid of the thieves and the hornets,"

Kamala said, smiling.

"Very clever of you," admitted Rajiv. "I admire your talent."

"And I admire your talent, Rajiv. You are as good as I am at cooking and cleaning. As long as you stay away from your friends at the barber shop and help me at harvest time, we just might live happily together after all."

The Pooka

AN ORIGINAL STORY BY J. M. KELLY

Irish Word:
Telly: television.

Tara O'Higgins lived in a house on a street with many other houses in the city of Dublin. She loved to play with her friends in the park and to go to the big cinemas on O'Connell Street.

But when school let out for summer holidays, Tara's favorite thing to do was to visit her grandparents in the Wicklow Mountains. Grandma and Grandpa lived on a farm that was surrounded by lots of hills, big and small. And out of the windows of the house you could see huge mountains rising in the distance.

Every summer Tara's mother drove Tara and her sister, Caitlin, to stay for a week with their grandparents. And this year the trip would be the best ever because Molly, Tara's best friend, was coming along.

"If we were to climb one of those hills," Molly said, "I'll bet you we could see the whole of Ireland."

Mrs. O'Higgins let the girls out of the car and told them to mind their Grandma and not cause any trouble.

"Do your chores around the farm. And Tara, look after your little sister, will you now?"

"Of course, Mama," Tara answered. The three girls waved as Mrs. O'Higgins drove away.

Grandma kissed each of the girls and made them sit right down to a snack of thick country bread and butter and cheese.

Afterward the girls ran out to look at the animals. The farm was small. Tara's grandfather was retired from his job with the government. He and Grandma kept a few sheep and one cow named Bessy. Their chickens were so friendly they would sit on the girls' shoulders. Except Caitlin was too scared and wouldn't let them.

The girls helped Grandma in the garden where she grew cabbages and potatoes and all kinds of flowers.

They carried hay and water for the cow and gathered the eggs from the hen house. They helped Grandpa fix a fence along the lane.

By the time evening came, the girls were hungry and tired. They ate a big supper and each had an extra helping of ice cream for dessert.

Afterward Molly whispered to Tara, "I don't see a telly here at all."

"No," Tara said. "Grandma and Grandpa don't watch television."

"What do they do to pass the time?"

"They read and tell stories and visit with their friends," Tara said. "You'll see. Grandpa has some fantastic stories."

The evening was a bit cool, so Grandpa built a fire in the fireplace. He used real turf, which he'd dug out of the ground himself last summer and dried. So much nicer, the girls agreed, than the silly little gas fireplace they had at home.

No sooner had Grandpa settled down in his rocking chair than he began to tell them a story: "This was in the old days, long before any of you lasses were born. I was attending a dance over in Ballyrush, don't you know. I had a grand time and even won a door prize, a big fat ham. Coming home late at night, I thought I would take a shortcut over Blackthorn Hill. I was halfway up the hill when I heard something behind me. I turned, and do you know what I saw?"

"What, Grandpa?" Tara asked.

"A dog bigger than a horse. And weren't his eyes glowing like hot coals? And his teeth this long. And he was coming right for me. I knew right off it was a pooka."

"What's a pooka?" Caitlin asked. She was clutching Tara's arm, hard.

"It's one of the spirits. It can take the shape of a dog or a horse or even an owl."

"What did you do?" the three girls asked together.

"What do you think? I ran for it. I was huffing and puffing up the hill as fast as I could go. But that pooka kept gaining on me. Then just as I could feel his breath on my neck, I stopped!"

Caitlin gasped with fright.

"I hated to do it, but I gave that pooka the ham I'd won. I had wandered into his region, and I had to pay him his tribute. Sure enough, that was what he was after. He gobbled up that ham in two bites and disappeared. Poof!"

"Is that true, Grandma?" Tara asked.

"Your grandpa has lots of stories about the banshees and the little people and the spirits and the pookas. They are just stories."

"And one's as true as the next," Grandpa said.

Grandma winked at the girls. Tara and Molly winked back, but little Caitlin was hiding her eyes.

Grandpa told some more stories. The girls went to bed and fell asleep thinking about pookas and fairies and all kinds of enchanted beings.

The next morning they went to town and helped Grandma with her shopping. Then Tara told Grandma she wanted to take Molly and Caitlin on a walk in the hills. Last year Grandma had gone with them, but this year Tara thought they were old enough to go alone.

"All right," Grandma said. "I'll pack you some sandwiches. But mind you don't go too far. And be back well before tea time."

"We will, Grandma," Tara promised.

The girls put their sandwiches in their backpacks and started walking along a farm lane that led back into the hills among the sheep fields.

The hills were beautiful that time of year. The prickly gorse bushes were blooming with their bright yellow flowers. The heather spread across the hills in shades of purple and rose.

"Why are there no trees here, the way there are in the parks at home?" Molly asked.

"The trees were cut down years ago," Tara said, "for making barrels and ships and things. That's why we don't have to worry about getting lost. We can always see where we are."

"I'm going to pick flowers," Caitlin said. She ran across the field, picking daisies and wild snapdragons.

The girls walked a long way, up and down the hills. At first the sun was bright and warm. Then clouds began to move in. By late afternoon they had walked over many rolling hills and come to the biggest hill they had seen so far.

"If we climb up there, we'll be able to look all the way to the sea, I bet," Molly said.

"That's Blackthorn Hill," Tara said, "the one where Grandpa said he saw the pooka."

"You believe that silly story?" Molly asked her.

"No, but—"

"I want to look at the sea," Caitlin chimed in.

Tara agreed to go up. The climb was hard work. Before they reached the top, clouds began to blow in from the sea. In Ireland the weather can change very quickly.

"I think it might rain," Tara said. "We should turn back."

"But we're almost there," Molly answered.

"Just a bit farther," Caitlin said. "Please, Tara."

Tara agreed. They trudged up the final distance to the very top of Blackthorn Hill and sat down to rest on the rocks.

"There's the sea!" Molly pointed.

The girls looked. They could make out a tiny bit of dark blue between two hills.

"We're almost in the clouds," Caitlin said.

She was right. The clouds were thick now and hanging so close it seemed they could reach up and touch them. A few drops of rain came spitting down.

"We'd better start down now for sure," Tara said.

"I'm hungry," Caitlin complained.

"Silly, do you want to stay here and get soaked to the skin?" asked Tara. "We can eat later."

As the girls started back down the hill, the heavy clouds dropped even further. Soon the fog was so thick they could barely see where they were going. No matter which direction they looked, all they could see was a grayish-white mist.

"Are we headed in the right direction?" Molly asked. "I thought we came from over there."

"I think it was this way," Tara said, "but I'm not entirely sure."

"I'm cold!" Caitlin said.

The rain kept coming down harder and harder. They plunged on through the thick fog.

"Look!" Molly said. Through the mist they could see the outline of a lean-to, a little shed in the middle of a field.

The rain was pouring down now. All three girls began to run to reach the shelter. However, before they had gone three steps, little Caitlin stepped into a hole and fell.

"Ow!" she cried. She rolled on the wet ground, clutching her ankle.

Tara tried to help her up, but Caitlin couldn't walk. The two older girls carried her to the lean-to. Now they were out of the rain, but they were all soaking wet and cold.

"What will we do?" Molly asked. "We don't know where we are and we don't know the way back."

"It could rain for days," Caitlin added. "I'm scared."

"I'll think of something," Tara said. "For now, let's eat our sandwiches. That will make us feel better."

Molly began unwrapping their sandwiches, and Tara helped Caitlin lie down on some straw along the back wall. Suddenly they heard a noise out in the fog, a low growl. Tara and Molly peeked around the edge of the lean-to.

"Look!" Molly whispered.

Tara peered through the mist. She could make out the form of an animal. It looked like a dog, the biggest dog she'd ever seen. It stood almost as tall as she did and had a wild, scraggly coat.

"What is it?" Caitlin asked. She couldn't see from her position on the straw.

"A pooka!" Molly said.

"Oh, no!" Caitlin covered her eyes.

"Give me a sandwich," Tara said to Molly.

"Why, what are you going to do?" Molly asked.

"Just give it to me."

Taking the sandwich, Tara walked out into the rain, right toward the strange beast. The animal backed up. Tara placed half the sandwich on the ground and stepped back. The huge dog came carefully forward. He sniffed the sandwich. Then he gobbled it right down.

Molly almost expected to see him disappear in a flash. But he didn't. Instead, Tara held out another piece of sandwich. The animal came closer and took the piece of sandwich from her hand.

Tara stepped back under the lean-to and offered the rest of the sandwich to the dog. The big dog hesitated. Then he came in out of the rain and ate the last bit of food. He shook himself, spraying water in all directions. Molly was huddling against the back of the lean-to. Caitlin was so scared she had her eyes shut. But Tara petted the dog and let it sniff her hand.

"He's not a pooka at all," Tara said. "He's an Irish wolfhound. We learned about them at school. They're the biggest dogs in the world."

"Why did you give him our food?" Molly asked.

"Don't you see? He belongs to somebody. If I make friends with him, he can lead the way back for help."

"You're so clever, Tara," Molly said. "Do you think it will work?"

"The rain's letting up a bit," answered Tara. "I'll try it." To the dog she said, "Go home, boy. Take me home."

The big dog cocked his head and looked at her.

Tara stepped out into the fog. "Let's go, boy," she said. Finally the dog trotted out, barked, and started across the hill. Tara followed, stepping carefully through the fog. The dog ran a little ahead, then stopped to make sure she was coming. "Good dog," she called.

Molly and Caitlin waited in the lean-to. They ate the other two sandwiches, but Caitlin was shivering, she was so cold. Her ankle hurt, but she would not cry—she was too grown-up for that, she felt.

"Are you sure it wasn't a pooka?" she asked Molly. "Maybe he's lured Tara out there in order to eat her!"

"Pookas are only in stories," Molly said. "Tara knows what she's doing."

However, as the rain kept falling and the sky grew darker, even Molly began to wonder if maybe strange spirits were lurking in the fog. All of a sudden they heard the sound of an engine and saw headlights. A farm truck emerged out of the mist.

Tara jumped out, wearing a yellow slicker that was too big for her. The farmer helped them lift Caitlin into the cab of the truck. Then they all climbed in and headed down the hill.

Tara told how the huge dog led her all the way to his home, which was on the other side of Blackthorn Hill.

"Mr. Doyle here knows Grandpa," she said. "He

agreed to give us a ride home." The girls thanked the old farmer.

"We should thank your dog too," Tara said. "What's his name anyway?"

"We call him Pooka," the farmer said.

He couldn't understand why all three of them broke out laughing.

Cloudberry Trifle

AN ORIGINAL STORY BY MARTHA JOHNSON

"Sonja!" Sonja's younger brother Eric rushed into the barn where she was milking their skinny cow. "The king's herald! He's here—in our village!"

"Nonsense." Sonja patted the cow's bony side and lifted the bucket of frothy milk. At least today there'd be enough milk to go all the way around the table. Weren't they in enough trouble without Eric making up stories?

Their father had died several years ago, and their mother supported the family by running a dress shop. But business was slow, and Sonja had two brothers and five sisters, all younger than she. Sonja gave the cow an extra pat. In three days' time the cow would have to be sold to pay the debt on her mother's tiny shop. There would be no milk then for Sonja's sisters and brothers, and no money to buy it. When winter came again to their village, they might not have enough to eat. And Eric was making up stories.

"The king's herald doesn't come to the poorest village in all of Norway," she said sternly, frowning at Eric. "Everyone knows that."

Eric opened his mouth, and a blaring trumpet sound came out. Sonja blinked, then shook her head. The blare hadn't come from Eric. It had come from the village square. She put the milk bucket down and ran outside, Eric right behind her.

"See, Sonja, I told you. See?"

Sonja shushed her brother. She must be dreaming. The king's herald, brass buttons gleaming, horn blasting, stood in the center of the tiny mountain village.

The herald gave a final blast and cleared his throat. "Hear ye, hear ye!" he shouted. His voice was raspy as a frog's. He must have shouted this message too many times. "His Majesty the King announces a royal contest. On the day after tomorrow there will be a grand competition to name a new chef for the king. All the chefs in the kingdom are to bring their best dishes to the governor's estate. The winner will be named the new Royal Chef!"

The herald looked around him at the poor village and the poorer people. "Not that anything good could come from a place like this," he muttered, and he marched away.

The villagers buzzed with excitement at the thought of the king himself visiting so near their poor village. Sonja didn't buzz, but a little shiver went through her. She wasn't rich, and she wasn't beautiful, but she could cook. Her Cloudberry Trifle was so light and so sweet it made you smile to think about it. The recipe was a family favorite, passed down from her grandmother—sponge cake, broken into bits the size of bread crumbs, mixed with berries, custard, and whipped cream. Just a taste would have you dancing in the street.

"I'll do it," Sonja muttered to herself. "Why shouldn't I? The king will love my Cloudberry Trifle. I'll be the king's chef, and Mother won't have to worry about how to feed the family this winter."

Sonja was up with the sun the next morning, as usual. She hurried down the dusty street to the market to buy cloudberries. But the barrel that was usually heaped with cloudberries was empty.

"No cloudberries today," the greengrocer said. "Maybe next week."

"But I need them today," Sonja said. "Even if I have to pick them myself."

The greengrocer's face grew red with laughter. "Everyone knows that picking cloudberries is a job for a mountaineer," he said. "It's not a job for a silly girl." Then the greengrocer became serious. "Besides," he said, "there are bears in those mountains. Big, hungry bears. Cloudberry picking is dangerous. Don't go there all by yourself."

Sonja tossed her head, sending her yellow braids flying. "We'll see about that," she said. "Maybe what everyone knows isn't always right."

Sonja ran back home and put on a shirt and an old pair of pants belonging to her brother Eric. She got a pail for the berries and then looked into the pantry for something to eat, just in case she got hungry on the way. The shelves were all empty, except for a bowl of yesterday's Cloudberry Trifle. Sonja wrapped the bowl in a towel and put it into the empty pail.

The path up the mountain was narrow and steep. Boulders blocked the way. The sun beat down on Sonja's head, making sweat trickle into her eyes. She leaned against a rock to rest, looking at how far she'd come and how far she still had to go.

She thought about Mama, working long hours in the shop. She remembered what the greengrocer had said. "I'm not a silly girl," she told a passing raven, and she kept on climbing.

Cloudberries grew on a narrow ledge near the top of a cliff. As she climbed over yet another rock in her way, Sonja bit her lip. What if there were no berries on the bushes? What if they were still green? Maybe she was doing all this work for nothing.

Finally she rounded the last bend in the path. The ground was covered with creeping cloudberry plants, glistening with rich, golden berries. All of a sudden Sonja didn't feel tired. She took out the wrapped bowl from the pail, put it on the ground nearby, got on her knees, and started to pick, the yellow juice staining her fingers as the berries plopped into the pail, sending up a heavenly aroma. In only a few minutes, it seemed, the pail was full.

"That was easy," Sonja said to a curious marmot who was helping himself to the berries. "Who says a girl can't do this?"

A low growl answered her. The marmot scurried

away, and Sonja turned, her heart pounding like a hammer. A huge bear filled the path. His black fur gleamed, and his yellow eyes were angry. Sonja rose slowly and took a step backward. The bear took a step forward.

"Nice bear," Sonja said soothingly. His sharp teeth made jagged points around his red tongue. She didn't see a stick or a rock or anything she could use to frighten him off.

The bear took another step toward her, and the sharp scent of bear overwhelmed the smell of cloudberries. Then Sonja saw the bowl of yesterday's Cloudberry Trifle just a few steps away. She inched her way to the bowl, picked it up, unwrapped it, and set it down in front of her.

"Nice bear," she crooned, stepping slowly backward. "Have some lovely Cloudberry Trifle."

The bear's growl deepened. He shuffled forward until he was almost on top of the bowl. Then he stopped. He sniffed. If it is possible for a bear to smile, he smiled. He buried his nose in the bowl, lapping up that Cloudberry Trifle.

Sonja didn't wait around to see if he danced. She grabbed the full pail, took to her heels, and raced down the mountain, the pail bouncing at her side.

Sonja reached home more tired than she'd ever been in her life. But her work wasn't done yet. She still had to bake the cake, whip the cream, and make the cloudberry sauce. It was very late when she finished. Sonja tumbled into bed next to her sisters and dreamed of being chef to the king and bringing home enough gold to buy three cows.

The next day Sonja put on her best dress. Carrying the bowl of Cloudberry Trifle, Sonja walked all the way to the next village, where the big house of the governor towered about the huts.

The gate was crowded with people trying to get into the contest. A captain of the guard in a splendid uniform checked each contestant in. Finally it was Sonja's turn.

"Please, sir," she said, her voice suddenly very small. "I'm here for the contest."

The captain shook his head. "No girls allowed in the contest. Next!"

Anger made Sonja's voice loud. "Wait a minute! What do you mean?"

The captain looked bored. "Men only," he said. "Everyone knows all the great chefs are men. Next!"

Sonja was pushed back into the crowd, clutching

the bowl. For just an instant she wanted to cry into the trifle. Then she got mad.

"So all the best chefs are men, are they?" she muttered. "We'll see about that."

Hurrying, juggling the bowl of trifle, Sonja raced home. She changed from her dress to Eric's best shirt and pants. She stuffed her long braids up under his cap. "There!" she said. "Now we'll see about that contest."

The line was still long, and the captain of the guard was still bored. "Name?" he asked.

"Eric," Sonja replied, crossing her fingers.

"Enter," he said, hardly looking at her.

The contest entries spread across a magnificent table. Sonja was herded into the huge hall with the other contestants. She barely had time to look at the wonderful paintings and fabrics around her before a rustle swept through the crowd. The king was coming!

Sonja had never seen the king up close before. He frowned at the table and looked as though his crown was giving him a headache. One of his counselors hovered behind him, pointing out this dish and that.

Slowly the king worked his way down the table. Sonja's heart sank. The other entries sat on fine china plates and in bright crystal dishes. Why would the king even look at something in a plain pottery bowl?

The king tasted this dish and that. Nothing took the frown from his face. Then he came to the Cloudberry Trifle.

The king took a small spoonful. Sonja held her breath and thought about three new cows and enough milk to go around. The king began to nod. He turned to murmur something to his counselor. The counselor cleared his throat importantly.

"The king wishes to see the chef who made the Cloudberry Trifle."

Sonja's knees were knocking together as she approached the table. The king took another bite. He began to smile.

"Excellent!" the king said. "Excellent! What is your name, my boy?"

"Eric, sir, Your Highness," Sonja stammered.

The captain of the guard poked her. "Bow your head when you speak to the king," he whispered.

Quickly Sonja bobbed her head in the best bow she could manage. Eric's cap tumbled off her head, and her long braids swung toward the floor. A horrified gasp came from the crowd. "A girl!" they murmured. "It's a girl!"

"Arrest this impostor!" the counselor said in an awful voice.

The captain of the guard grabbed Sonja by both arms. "What is your real name?" he demanded.

"Sonja," she said loudly. "My name is Sonja."

"Throw her out," the counselor began, "and—"

"Now wait a minute." The king licked his spoon. He looked as if his headache had vanished. "Let's not be hasty. She does make a superb Cloudberry Trifle."

"But, Your Majesty," the counselor said, "you can't have a girl for a chef. Everyone knows all the great chefs are men."

All the people gathered in the big hall were silent. The king looked at Sonja. Then he looked at the half-empty bowl of Cloudberry Trifle. Sonja thought his feet moved as though they wanted to dance.

"Maybe what everyone knows isn't always right." The king helped himself to another spoonful. He danced a step or two. Then he cleared his throat and spoke in a loud voice.

"Mistress Sonja is hereby declared the Royal Chef. Cloudberry Trifle will henceforth be known as the Royal Dessert. Let everyone know that!"

Maya's Stone Soup

ADAPTED BY BRUCE LANSKY
FROM A EUROPEAN FOLKTALE

Spanish Words:

Burro (pronounced "BOO-ro"): a small donkey.

Adobe (pronounced "a-DO-beh"): means "constructed of mud."

Tortillas (pronounced "tor-TEE-yas"): round pancake-like
bread made from corn.

Fiestas (pronounced "fee-YES-tas"): means "festivities."

Loca (pronounced "LO-ka"): means "crazy."

Deliciosa (pronounced "de-lee-SYO-sa"): means "delicious."

Gracias (pronounced "GRA-tsias"): means "thank you."

Por favor (pronounced "POR fa-Vor"): means "please."

Maya had spent a rain-soaked weekend with her
grandparents, who lived on a mountain farm in

Guatemala. It was summer, the rainy season. Maya had gathered eggs from the hens. She had milked the cows. She had fed the pigs and watched them roll around in the mud. She had helped her grandmother care for a brand-new colt. But she was totally unprepared for what she would discover when she went back to her home on the coast of the Pacific Ocean.

On Sunday afternoon, Maya rode her burro down the winding mountain road, through the rain, toward home. As she got closer to her village, Maya saw that the road was covered with water. Straw and tile roofs had been blown off the houses. Debris was scattered everywhere. All along the way people were busy cleaning up and repairing their *adobe* houses. Maya guessed that a great hurricane had devastated the area while she was away.

As she rode on, Maya became more and more worried about what she'd find when she got back to her village. Were her parents and her little brother and sister safe? Was her house ruined? Maya was anxious to be home to help her family.

Suddenly her burro stumbled over something in the muddy road. Maya reined in the burro and climbed down to see whether it was hurt. After she made sure that the burro was all right, Maya took a stick and poked around in the mud to see what had tripped it.

After a short search, Maya found a big, round stone. She rolled it into a puddle to clean it off. The stone was a beautiful reddish-brown color and it sparkled enchantingly. Maya wondered whether the stone might be valuable and decided to take it home to show her family.

Maya put the beautiful stone in her saddlebag, climbed back up on the burro, and continued to ride home through the mud and water. By the time she arrived, she wasn't surprised at what she saw. The hard-packed dirt floor of the house was completely covered with water. The shutters were gone, and the wind had blown rain in through the windows. Maya's parents were bone tired—they'd been up through the night bailing the water out of the house. Her little brother, Tomas, and her sister, Gabriela, were sitting in front of the house, crying.

"Maya, you're back! Thank goodness," exclaimed her mother. "Please take care of your brother and sister while we get the water out of the house. See if you can find them something to eat."

Maya looked for something to eat. The rain had poured through the kitchen window, soaking the tortillas in the cupboard. The chicken coop had been blown away; there were no eggs or chickens to cook. The garden was flooded. All the food was either gone or destroyed. Tomas and Gabriela were crying—cold and hungry. Maya had to do something. But what?

Hoping to borrow some food, Maya ran to the next-door neighbors. Their house was in worse shape than Maya's. When she asked for something to eat, they said, "Can't you see that we're busy fixing our house? Ask someone else!"

With the sound of her brother's and sister's crying ringing in her ears, Maya ran down the road to where a house used to be. It was gone. All that was left were some wooden planks, a bed, a table, and a chair sitting in a large puddle of water. A goat was nibbling on what used to be the vegetable garden. The neighbors were sitting on the bed, red-eyed and bewildered. They had lost almost everything. Maya didn't even bother to ask them for food. They needed help more than she did.

After trying a few more neighbors, Maya realized that everyone was too busy to care about her problems. She needed a new idea. When she got back home, she noticed her mother's big, black pot behind the house. It must have floated out the back door. Maya's mother used this huge pot when grandparents, uncles, aunts, and cousins all gathered for *fiestas*.

Maya picked up the pot and carried it toward the house. She thought she might cook something hot and nutritious for Tomas and Gabriela. But what? Slowly a plan began to take shape in her mind. "This could work…" she thought.

"Tomas! Gabriela! Come here. I need your help," Maya called.

Her brother and sister came running out of the house. They weren't crying anymore. They were glad to have a chance to help. "What can we do?" asked Tomas.

"I want you to look for anything dry enough to burn: paper, sticks, pieces of wood—anything," Maya told them. "We're going to make a fire."

"What for?" asked little Gabriela.

"So we can cook some soup in this pot."

Tomas and Gabriela smiled at the thought of finally getting some food.

"What kind of soup?" asked Tomas.

"Stone soup," Maya answered. "I found a very

beautiful stone on the way from our grandparents' house. I'll put it in when the water is boiling. If you've never tasted stone soup before, you're in for a treat."

Tomas shrugged and pointed to his head with his finger. Then he twirled it around a few times. "Maya's gone *loca*," he cracked. Gabriela started giggling.

After finding a dry box of matches in the kitchen, a spoon, and a knife, Maya carried the pot to the small stone fireplace outside the house where her mother usually cooked. While waiting for Tomas and Gabriela to come back with paper and wood, Maya scouted for dry sticks and twigs and started a little fire.

But instead of helping Maya, Tomas and Gabriela ran off giggling to their parents. "Mamá, Papá, something's wrong with Maya. She's gone *loca!*"

Maya's parents looked up from their work. "What are you talking about?"

"We haven't had anything to eat in hours, so what is she cooking? Stone soup!"

Their parents shrugged and went back to work. They had too much work to worry about what Maya was cooking. Besides, Tomas and Gabriela weren't crying anymore.

When they realized their parents were too busy to

pay attention to them, Tomas and Gabriela ran off to the neighbors' houses spreading the word: "Maya's gone *loca!* She's cooking stone soup!"

By the time Tomas and Gabriela returned, without any firewood, Maya had a good fire going and the pot was filled with water from the well.

But Tomas and Gabriela were not alone. A few neighbors had followed them back to see crazy Maya and her stone soup. Maya's parents interrupted their work to see what was going on.

"Tomas, Gabriela, hurry. I need more wood. You need a hot fire to cook stone soup." The children scurried off to find some firewood.

"Are you really cooking stone soup?" asked a curious neighbor.

"Of course," Maya answered. "It's an old family recipe, and very *deliciosa*. When it's cooked, I'll give you a taste." Maya's parents looked at each other and shrugged, wondering what she was up to.

When Tomas and Gabriela had returned with armfuls of dry wood, Maya built up the fire. Then she held up her stone for everyone to see. "Here is the most important ingredient. See how beautiful it is?" Then she dropped it into the kettle. The stone splashed when it hit the water and clanked when it hit the bottom. Maya began to stir the soup.

After a few minutes, she dipped a spoon into the kettle and tasted the soup. "Not bad!" she said. "But it needs a little seasoning."

"I'll go and get some," said a curious neighbor. She ran home and returned in a few minutes with a small bag of salt and a peppermill.

Maya sprinkled salt and ground some pepper into the soup. Then she stirred the soup a few times, dipped her spoon into the soup, and tasted it. "That's a little better! But I think it could use a few carrots."

"I'll see if I can find a few in our garden," said another neighbor.

When he returned with some carrots, Maya cut off the greens, washed the carrots, and threw them into the pot. Then she stirred the soup for a few minutes and took a taste. "Mmmm! It's coming along nicely. But I think it could use some potatoes."

"I'll see if I can dig some up," said an old man who worked on a farm nearby. When he returned with some potatoes, Maya washed them, chopped them into small pieces, and tossed them into the pot. Then she stirred the soup and tasted it again. "Now it's starting to taste good," she said. "But still…it could use a little more flavor. Maybe an onion or two…"

"No problem," said the local innkeeper. "I can spare a few."

"…and a chicken," continued Maya.

"I'll catch one," called out a farmer whose chickens had survived the hurricane.

When the innkeeper returned with the onions and the farmer returned with the chicken, Maya cleaned the onions, plucked and washed the chicken, and tossed everything into the soup. Then she stirred the soup and let it simmer.

While everybody waited for the soup to cook, some villagers arrived with guitars and began to play. The mood turned festive. People gathered around the pot and sang.

When she thought the soup was ready, Maya took a final taste. *"Deliciosa!"* she announced. "Now, anyone who brings a bowl and a spoon can have a taste of my stone soup."

The onlookers watched as Tomas and Gabriela ran to the kitchen. They returned with bowls and spoons, out of breath.

Gabriela was first. After her bowl was full, she took

a taste. "Mmmm mmmm! *Deliciosa. Gracias,* Maya."

Tomas was impatient. He held out his bowl and clanked it with his spoon. "Can I have some stone soup, *por favor?*"

"Of course," Maya answered as she ladled out some soup into his bowl.

He slurped it down rapidly. "*Gracias!* May I have more, *por favor?*"

In a few minutes the crowd of villagers headed home to get bowls and spoons. When they returned, the hungry crowd had doubled or tripled. Almost everyone in the village had come for a bowl of stone soup—even the mayor.

When all the soup was gone, the mayor made a brief speech: "I want to thank Maya for feeding us and cheering us up at a time when we all needed it." Everyone cheered Maya, who took a little bow.

"And I'd like to thank you," Maya told the gathered crowd. "My stone soup would not have been quite so delicious without your help. And if anyone here is ever hungry, I'll be happy to loan you my soup stone. I think you know the recipe."

Annie and the Black Cat

AN ORIGINAL STORY BY HELEN RAMES BRIGGS

English Words:

Cracksman (pronounced "KRAKS-man"): means "burglar."

Bobby: an English term for "police officer."

Scalawags (pronounced "SKA-la-wags"): means "rascals."

Blunderbuss (pronounced "BLUNDER-bus"): a type of rifle.

Scrape, scrape, scrape. Annie, the scullery maid, barely older than a child, was scraping the steps with a block of sandstone. It was a fine house. The bronze knocker on the door gleamed, and the windows sparkled in the early morning sun.

The year was 1871, in London, England.

The steps gleamed white as Annie scrubbed them down. Her head down, the harsh rasp of the sandstone filled her ears. At first she did not hear the faint, pitiful meow. Then suddenly she heard. Annie shifted her knees. A little, gaunt black cat was looking at her. Its big eyes seemed to plead. It came close and rubbed against her patched boots.

"Oh," thought Annie, "the little creature is hungry—how poor and thin he is. What shall I do?" To feed him would mean instant dismissal. With no character reference. Mrs. Chumbly, the cook, would see to that. Bush, the butler, wasn't as mean as Mrs. Chumbly, but he would also not want a cat in the house. Annie shuddered; she knew what losing her job without reference meant. Either starvation or returning to her family home. And her folks were the poorest of the poor, with too many mouths to feed already.

The cat pressed close to Annie. Its bony ribs quivered. Annie scrubbed with little jerks. She must think; there must be a way to feed the little animal. How could she carry the cat into her attic room?

Then Annie saw the box full of cleaning rags and polishes sitting on the steps. Quickly she placed the cat in the box and covered him with the rags.

"Be quiet," she whispered. Up the back stairs she scuttled until, breathless, she reached her attic room. "Emma will be givin' me a bit of toast and some milk. No meows until I get back or there'll be real trouble!"

The cat seemed to understand. Only a faint purring sounded as Annie tucked him under her ragged quilt.

Annie firmly shut her door and raced down the stairs. She had to lay the fire, set the breakfast table in the servants' hall, cook the eggs, and make the tea.

Emma, the house maid, her only friend, looked at her sharply. "Ye're winded," she observed. "It's almost 'alf past eight. Let's eat now. Mrs. Chumbly and Bush are upstairs with the missus."

The two girls sat down and began their meal, but Annie was too excited to eat. "Emma, I must tell ye. I found me a black cat. He's almost starved. How can I keep him hid and fed without Mrs. Chumbly knowin' or tellin' the gentry?"

Emma replied in a shocked tone of voice. "Ye know what'll 'appen if Chumbly finds out about a cat! She is so mean, she'll run upstairs to the missus and out ye'll be in the street with no recommendation."

Annie's eyes glistened with tears. "I'll just be feedin'

the poor little one for a few days. It's so thin and starved."

Emma shrugged her shoulders, then said, "I 'ave the upstairs cleanin' today. I'll sneak a cup o' milk and some crumbs into your room right now, before old Chumbly and Bush come down to the kitchen."

After the quick breakfast, Emma scurried away with the food. She was just in time, for Mrs. Chumbly came grumbling into the scullery.

"Where's my breakfast, ye lazy kitchen wench?" she asked, her beady eyes gleaming. "What, the dishes not finished? Ye lazy good-for-nothin'!" She brought her fist cracking down on the table. "Here I be fixin' six-course dinners and eight-course suppers, and a smear o' greasy platters is starin' me in the eye. Next time it 'appens, up ye go to see the missus. She'll give ye the sack, or my name ain't Chumbly."

Trembling, Annie plunged the dishes into the hot suds, washed them, and placed them in the drying rack. She then set the table and served breakfast to Mrs. Chumbly.

"Get on wi' it," snarled Mrs. Chumbly as she smeared jam on her toast. "Peel them parsnips, do them potatoes…"

Annie was silent as she worked. She stirred the caper sauce, basted the mutton, and so it went. But all through the endless hours of that day, all of her thoughts were on the black cat.

"What a dear black un' he is," she thought. "Emma must have given him his milk. By now, the little un' must be asleep in my bed."

At last she was through for the day. She lit a candle and wearily crept upstairs. Yes, there the cat was, sleeping on her bed. He opened one eye as she crawled onto the lumpy mattress.

"Shhhh," breathed Annie. "We'll be safe here for a while." A faint purr came from the black cat's throat. Soon they were both sleeping the sleep of exhaustion.

Annie rose promptly at half past five. One of her duties was cleaning out the dead embers in the kitchen range. The wooden sticks were damp today and the fire was slow to start. The water for the tea did not boil, so the master's breakfast was delayed.

The master was in a bad mood. His fingers drummed impatiently on the table as he waited for a hot cup of tea.

The delay made him late for work. Finally he stormed out of the house. Alas, Annie was below the steps, near the cellar door, talking to the milkman. She had pressed a shilling into his hand and hidden in her apron a small bottle of milk.

The master saw Annie. How dare his kitchen maid speak to a tradesman? Only the cook was allowed this privilege.

"What is going on down there?" he bellowed. The milkman, with one glance at the master's red face, fled. Annie did likewise, carrying the concealed bottle to her attic room.

The master pounded on his front door, which Bush, the butler, opened with a proper look of concern.

"Do you know what I discovered?" demanded the master. "A scullery maid speaking with a tradesman. I will not have this in my establishment. I know the burglaries that take place constantly are aided and abetted by the idle gossip of servants. Tell each and every servant that it will mean instant dismissal if such behavior is observed. No one except the cook is to speak with tradespeople."

"Yes, sir," replied Bush humbly. The master left for work in a fury.

Bush did as he was ordered. He began at the top, telling the mistress' ladies' maid, then the house maid, and last, Annie.

He said to each one, "No conversation with anyone. Cook alone can see the watercress man, the rabbit skinman, the butcher, the fishmonger, and the milkman."

He looked sharply at Annie, but showed a little sympathy by not saying that she was the guilty one—the one who had occasioned the master's outburst.

As Annie left the room to go back into the kitchen, Mrs. Chumbly screamed, "Ye dolly-mop. If I catch ye laggin' one more time, I will take ye to the master and missus. Then out ye'll go." And her sharp words followed Annie, ringing in her ears.

In the kitchen Annie peeled the parsnips, with downcast eyes. Her thoughts were in a whirl. In all the gray days of her life she had never had anybody or anything to love. Inside her, a slow anger began to burn, but years of being a scullery maid had taught her to say nothing. Why couldn't she have one black cat?

Just then, with a slight scurry, a mouse ran over her foot. Yes, the kitchen had mice—even rats. They sprang out from behind the range, the cupboards, and the pantry, mostly at night.

Annie began to see a faint glimmer of hope. Cats

catch mice!

When the house was silent and all was dark, the outer doors locked and the inner doors latched by Bush, the master and mistress sleeping soundly, and the servants in bed, Annie took the black cat, and oh-so-quietly crept down the outer stairs. She stopped; she listened; and then she released the cat when she reached the kitchen.

"Catch some mice, my pretty one," she whispered. "I'll be down to get ye before the clock strikes one."

And so it was that every night the black cat caught mice. He grew plump. In the daytime he stayed in Annie's attic room under the eaves. Strangely enough, he seemed to know that he must be quiet, so he spent the daylight hours sleeping in a parsnip crate or under Annie's quilt.

Meanwhile, some villains were planning to rob the master's fine house. A great many homes of the wealthy gentry were robbed, because many of the poor took to crime as a way of life.

A cracksman named Joe and his companion, Climbin' Jerry, had spent weeks planning the crime. They knew when the neighborhood bobby made his nightly rounds. Joe, masquerading as a fishmonger, had been courting Mrs. Chumbly. First he talked to her in her kitchen. Then he asked her to go out with him on her day off. Mrs. Chumbly, being a rawboned, homely widow, was flattered and pleased by Joe's attentions. The cracksman was a handsome man.

Joe was also clever. He took weeks getting his information, but by smart questioning, he soon knew the layout of the house; the types of bolts and locks on all the outer and inner doors; and, most important, where the family's silver was kept.

Mrs. Chumbly had bragged one day, "We 'ave five tea services, silver coffeepots, and five candelabras. 'Tis a sight, the beauty of it all. And safe too. It's in a closet, with such locks ye can't believe."

"And where might such treasure be kept?" asked Joe mildly. "T'ain't safe anywhere with such scalawags aroun' and about."

"Oh, yes, 'tis," answered Mrs. Chumbly proudly. "I told the master to put it in my pantry behind an iron door, an' 'e thought that it was such a good idea, 'e gave me a spot of money. He ain't such a bad lot. No cracksman would ever look in my pantry! I know it well." She giggled happily.

So, after many weary weeks, Joe knew what he

wished to know. He and Climbin' Jerry were ready.

The night was pitch black and quiet. The stillness was broken only by the footsteps of the bobby as he made his rounds. Two dark shadows crept to the back of the fine house. They carried a huge carpetbag.

"Be keerful o' them tools," Joe whispered to Climbin' Jerry. "Now, quickly, before the bobby comes back, shimmy up that pipe, break a pane, let ye'erself in, and open the front door when I whistle like a bird."

Up the pipe went Jerry (he wasn't called Climbin' Jerry for nothing). Carefully he took an instrument and pried open a pane of glass. He caught the glass, slipped a hand inside the window, and drew the bolt.

He waited but didn't hear a sound. Again he listened, but heard nothing.

In his stockinged feet Jerry slipped inside. He lit his lantern. The light revealed that he was in the library. Slowly he opened the library door. Before him, a long hall stretched to the front door. He crept forward and drew the bolt. Again he paused. Then, with his tool, he ground a hole around the lock, then another hole. The lock opened.

A shrill bird call struck his ears. He quickly opened the door and Joe slipped in. They closed the door gently. They were just in time, for the sound of heavy footfalls fell upon their ears. The bobby was passing on his rounds.

"Douse the light," whispered Joe.

They stood, not moving, scarcely breathing. Only heavy snoring could be heard in the pitch-black house.

"It's time," whispered Joe. "To the kitchen and the pantry. With no light, we gotta feel with our hands. Hand me the cutter."

In the pantry Joe thrust the cutter into the keyhole of the iron door. He swung his full weight against the cutter. Over and over it ground, but the locks would not give. Jerry took his turn, but still nothing happened. The men were clammy with sweat.

Suddenly there was a lurch, a faint metallic peeping. The cracksman threw his weight against the door. The locks gave way, and the door swung open.

There, before their delighted eyes, stood row upon row of rich, gleaming silver. Swiftly the two villains filled the two sacks taken from the carpetbag. When the bags were filled, Joe and Jerry listened. They heard nothing but the ticking of a clock and a slight scurrying. Swiftly they passed into the kitchen and made their way toward the front hall and the unlatched door.

Suddenly the cracksman stepped on something soft that moved. "Yowee-yow-ee-yow-ee," screeched the black cat. His tail was under Joe's foot.

Sharp claws dug in the cracksman's leg. The cat jerked his tail loose. A whirlwind of fury enveloped Joe. He dropped the sack; Climbin' Jerry tripped over it in the dark and sprawled on the floor.

The cat continued to screech. Lights blazed. Running footsteps came toward the burglars. The entire household was awake!

The master stood in the hall, a blunderbuss in his hands. Bush appeared in the door of the breakfast room, wagging a huge pistol menacingly.

"We have them!" cried the master. "Call the bobbies, Bush. These scoundrels have been caught in the act of burglary."

Joe rubbed his scratched face. Jerry lay flat on the floor groaning. The black cat hissed and spat.

When the bobbies had come and gone with the two burglars, the master, looking a mite foolish in his nightcap and nightshirt, decided to ask a question. The servants stood in a circle, shaking with cold and excitement.

The master pointed a lean finger. "Who does yon

cat belong to? Speak up! To whom does he belong?"

White of face and trembling with fear, Annie came forward. Her teeth were chattering when she said, "Oh, m-m-m-master, sir, 'tis my b-b-b-black cat. He's a fine mouser."

"Do not be fearful, girl," said the master. "I am grateful to your mouser, if that is what he is. He defended our home and saved our silver."

"Kind sir, may I keep my black cat?" asked Annie, wiping tears from her eyes.

"Yes, you may," said the master. "And," he added, turning to his wife, "there should be some other reward for the girl. Don't you agree?"

"Oh, yes," replied his wife. "I will be needing a ladies' maid soon. Clara will be leaving to marry."

"Good," said the master, rubbing his hands together. "Consider it done. You, Annie, will be my dear wife's ladies' maid." Looking at Mrs. Chumbly, whose face was white because she had recognized Joe, the master added, "Cook will have to make do with some other girl."

Thus Annie kept her black cat, which caught any mice that dared to come near that fine house. The mistress of the house was kind and generous, so Annie spent many a comfortable year with her. It was as though a fine dream had come true: Annie had a pet to love, and a home where she could be happy.

AUTHOR BIOGRAPHIES

Helen Rames Briggs lives in Glendale, California. She has one son, two grandchildren, and three great-grandchildren. For many years, Helen was in the retail book business, but from an early age she had acquired an interest in writing, to which she has devoted much of her time. She has published more than fifty articles, poems, and, especially, children's stories. She is the author of one book, *The Quinducklets*. Her story, "Annie and the Black Cat," is original.

Martha Johnson is the author of three novels, as well as a number of short stories that have been published in such magazines as *Jack and Jill, Pennywhistle Press, Young American, Teen, YM, Tiger Beat*, and others. She lives on a farm in Pennsylvania and is currently working on her next novel. Her stories, "Coudberry Trifle" and "Hidden Courage," are original.

Jack Kelly is the author of a number of books for children, including a biography of Benjamin Franklin and an adaptation of stories by Washington Irving. He lives in New York's Hudson Valley, the scene of Irving's famous tale "Rip Van Winkle." Jack is also the author of three novels for adults, including *Mad Dog*, an account of the bank robber John Dillenger. Jack has written about business and history for many magazines. His story, "The Pooka," is original.

Bruce Lansky enjoys writing funny poems for children (the most popular of which are in *Poetry Party, Kids Pick the Funniest Poems, A Bad Case of the Giggles*, and *New Adventures of Mother Goose)*, and he loves to perform in school assemblies and workshops. Before he started to write children's books, Lansky wrote humorous books for parents and baby name books. He has two grown children and currently lives with his computer near a beautiful lake in Minnesota. His stories, "Kamala and the Thieves," "Sarah's Pickle Jar," and "Maya's Stone Soup" are all adapted from folktales.

Joanne Mitchell lives in Rochester, New York, with her husband. Their two sons are both college students. Joanne graduated from MIT with a Ph.D. in chemistry and now works as a technical writer. She has had short stories published in *Isaac Asimov's Science Fiction Magazine* and in *Aboriginal Science Fiction Magazine*. In addition to reading and writing, Joanne enjoys baking bread, hiking, canoeing, and sea kayaking. She also practices t'ai chi every day. Her story, "Emily and the Underground Railroad," is original.

Stephen Mooser has written more than fifty books for children, ranging from picture books, such as *The Ghost with the Halloween Hiccups*, to nonfiction, such as *Into the Unknown: Nine Astounding Stories*, to novels, such as *Elvis Is Back and He's in the Sixth Grade!*, as well as two chapter-book series, *The Creepy Creature* books and the *All-Star Meatballs* books. He has recently finished *Maid Marian's Adventures in Sherwood Forest* , the first novel in the *Girls to the Rescue* series. A former filmmaker and treasure hunter, Stephen's adventures have made their way into many of his books. Currently President of the Society of Children's Book Writers and Illustrators, he has two children, Chelsea and Bryn, and lives in Los Angeles, California. His story, "Young Maid Marian and her Amazing, Astounding Pig," is original.

Anne Schraff currently lives in Spring Valley, California. As a small child, Anne traveled all over America with her brother and widowed mother. Her mother's courage served as a shining example that encouraged Anne to pursue her dream of becoming a writer. As she watched her mother pull their trailer over the mountains, change tires, and do carpentry and electrical work on their cabin, Anne knew that just as her mom let nothing stand in her way, so would nothing ever stop her either. Her story, "Bai and the Tree of Life," is original.

Perform a *Girls to the Rescue* Play!

Now you can produce *Girls to the Rescue* plays at school using scripts and materials from Baker Plays. Please call (617) 482-1280 for more information.